SPRAY THE BEES

By

Daniel Jared Halpern

Spray the Bees

ISBN 978-0-9889102-0-1

To the Flower I could never pick

◯

SHE GLARED AT ME FROM THE CORNER OF THE HIVE where the walls formed an angle. Her age was imperceptibly timeworn yet the atmosphere she created was full of spirit and forward-thinking. I sat there looking back at her from the edge of the hive when the gatherers were swarming back in with the day's harvest. I had already gathered my nectar today and so I sat for a few moments relaxing my overworked body. The worker continued to look at me as if she was reading my character by merely observing the pace of my breath. Soon, she turned her head slowly away from me, out yonder to the sun that was setting in the distance. Despite all the noise of buzzing and flapping down to the hive, I remained focused on the old worker.

As the crowd rushed to the hive, some of them carelessly bumped into me as they passed by. Each nudge pushed me closer and closer to falling down as I remained focused on the old worker who was unaffected by the rapid flow of workers retiring to the hive for the night. Suddenly I lost my grip on the smooth white wall and fell down into the dark hive with my wings rushing to support my nectar filled body. My wings tried to yank me back up, but my efforts were hindered because of the immense flow of bees into the hive looking for their combs. I was pushed down to the inner walls of the hive and put away my wings for when I actually could use them. I started to crawl miserably down toward my comb where I needed to retire for the night like all of the other workers.

I stopped for a second and looked up to the entrance of the hive where the light was fleeing as the lid was closing over us. With a *slam* we were covered in darkness. I crawled up and over one sheet of the hive to my cell which looked so rejuvenating at that moment. Now it was time to digest the nectar and pass it on to my colleagues for it to be processed into honey.

Fatigue rolled through my body as I collapsed into my cell. Rose and Charlie, my two honey processors, arrived within moments of me beginning to relax in my cell. They pulled me out of my cell with reluctant effort and began extracting the nectar from my honey sack. I sat there motionless as this was done as I could not wait to retreat to my cell at once. Soon they had taken all of the nectar necessary to make the next batch of their honey and so they left me on the comb wall, helpless. I had a hard time getting back up. My body was already asleep but my mind was in a perpetual insomnia. Somehow I found my way back to my cell and lost consciousness instantly.

When I awoke I thought that I had risen from an eternal grave. Slowly my strength returned to my body and I opened my eyes to once again see the world that I was living in. My vision finally came into focus. I crept out of my cell with gallant haste and fluttered my wings. The hive was still in darkness except for the dim light that was piercing through the round holes of the white walls. These spotlights shined on the honey-combs all around where workers were getting up to tend to the day's labor. Before long I could see the magnitude of activity on the surface of the combs. Bees were navigating through the constant traffic, finding their way to their jobs throughout the hive.

My job, though initially complete, was never quite done, as it were, because *a bee is always busy*. By instinct I was compelled to visit the Queen's Lair for work that needed to be done. I looked around for the fastest route to the lair but all paths were filled with equivocal traffic. Somehow I was able to shift myself into the flow of moving bees on my way to the lair. I walked with an agitated step to the tune of hundreds of other bees pushing and shoving me in the same direction.

I passed various departments on the way to the lair. The honey producing and filling department had bees rapidly working to fill all empty cells with honey. This was being done en masse which made it difficult for me to spot my two close colleagues, Rose and Charlie. Though I was moving rather fast along the path to the lair, I knew well the process of filling the combs with honey. The workers regurgitate the honey into the empty cells and then cap them off with wax to seal them for use later. I could always see some bees break-ing into the finished honeycombs, eating the sweet honey for lunch.

I also passed several bees spread out in the middle of the hive where they were fanning their wings rapidly.

These workers were producing a wind that kept the hive cool as our activity increased. I always thought that their job was cumbersome and realistically menial but I would always be thankful for their work as it may be quite necessary to the survival of our colony.

As my eyes wandered across the business of other bees, the traffic continually pushed me back into line as we reached the Queen's Lair. The entrance of the lair was protected by warriors who kept a disciplined watch on all of us who entered. Instantly the Queen was visible and the bees in the traffic spread out around her. All of us crawled close to her with our utmost respect and began licking her to receive the daily pheromones to pass on to the entire hive. These pheromones that the Queen produced were a reminder to the bees of the hive that the Queen was still alive and that they should act accordingly to suit her needs and continue to produce. The Queen was pleasured by our constant devotion and attention to her. She then motioned for the bees in front of her to move aside as she waddled gracefully over to some nearby empty cells. She placed her abdomen into each one, filling them with transparent white larvae. Next to these new nests were wax covered combs that held sleeping larvae pupae which would soon hatch into new worker bees to be placed into the workforce. Our job became ostensive: to seal off the new nests with wax just behind the Queen over the baby larvae.

We got to work capping the larvae cells, working alongside each other in a social manner. The workers filling the caps began to talk regularly, however they could not say anything adverse about the Queen in her presence. Two workers waved their antennae at each other.

"Say, you think we will see any new *packages* anytime soon?" One buzzed to the other. She was referring to the Queen laying a larva with Royal Jelly injected into it which would make it capable of becoming the new Queen.

"Well I heard that *somebody* is busy *getting to work* at a nearby colony, if you know what I mean," the other buzzed back. The first bee leaned in close to the other and whispered nearly inaudibly.

"Do you mean the Queen is going to go off to mate at the Adriana Hive?!"

"Shhh, don't be so loud! Yes of course, but you didn't hear it from me," the other whispered back. They both looked over to the Queen who was walking relatively far away from them, planting the larvae with a winsome smile on her face.

I shook my head at the gossip precipitated by the workers. I hastily finished my job and walked away. Gossip like this only created hysteria at the hive. Whenever the Queen would leave or make an announcement that she was leaving the hive for a period of time, all of the bees would blather gossip about her and create rumors that caused hundreds of bees to swarm around the hive in circles for no better reason than the Queen is going out for a snack, or something along those lines. I did not have the thirst for such buffoonery, yet I did not think myself greater than any other bee by not joining the swarm. I would much rather do my job and get by so that I am protected and life goes according to plan.

Now that I finished my work, I thought that I might go for a stroll over to the Public Porch at the foot of the hive to breathe some fresh air. As the morning traffic began to dissipate, I walked freely down toward the bottom of the hive. All was normal and peachy until I glanced over at a bee standing alone in front of a light porthole on the side of the white wall where bright light was beaming in onto him. It was a handsome Drone who was looking outward to the beauty of the world outside. He looked so strong and collected as he stared motionless through the round porthole of the hive. I was too embarrassed to get close to him so I hid myself behind a mound of wax that was covering several combs housing the baby larvae.

Suddenly an alien buzzing sound came out of no-where. The Drone gently paced a few steps backward as a bee swooped in through the porthole. I was honestly shocked to see who it was that arrived. It was the Queen of the Luna Hive herself in the flesh! She landed right in front of the Drone and looked at him with a smile dripping with passionate lust and affection. The Drone, though startled as he was, must have been expecting her all this time and neared close to her gently. The young Queen Luna tipped her head toward the Drone and passionately began kissing him. I lifted my head slowly above the mound to see both of them beginning to mate. After a while I could not watch much more and looked away. Before long, they were finished and I could hear them talking to each other fervently.

"When will I see you again?" the Drone asked Queen Luna.

"Soon, but my hive will not allow me another holiday once I return...at least for a while." The young Queen appeared to love the Drone very much and was disappointed that she had to tend to the public life of Queen of the Luna Hive. Queen Luna then gave the Drone a final kiss and flew off through the porthole back to her hive. I looked back at the Drone who appeared to have felt like he had been touched by an angel. The Drone started walking away almost in my direction so I quickly dipped my head down behind the mound hoping that he did not see me spying on his business with the famed Queen of a foreign hive.

Once the Drone had finally passed and faded into the hive, I raised my head back up with a sigh of relief. Arbitrarily, the mound that I was hiding behind popped open with a newborn bee that pushed me out of the way and walked off to start its life.

I recounted the events that had just occurred and began walking again towards the bottom of the hive because now I *really* needed some fresh air.

I reached the bottom of the hive where the light was gleaming from all four sides of the walls. I saw where many bees were conversing and I fluttered out of the hive onto the Public Porch.

The full exposure to the morning light caused my eyes to adjust and prospect the wooden porch and the bees all around me. Everyone was bustling by as many bees were leaving the hive to forage for nectar. As I looked up to see the beautiful blue sky and tree leaves hanging above us, some yellow pollen fell into my eyes and all around from some homecoming bees who had residual pollen dropping from their legs. I wiped the pollen off of myself and looked back down to the porch. As usual, the warrior bees were guarding the entrance to the hive on the Public Porch with their arms folded and their eyes surveying the area for wrongdoings and wrongdoers. I strolled by everyone, breathing in the fresh summer air and eavesdropping on the public chatter of the porch. No one had anything extraordinary to say but all the talking created a homey feeling of patriotism within me. I live in a great hive with great bees, I thought. As I thought these pleasant things, I looked over at my fellow bees walking in and out of the hive's entrance.

Soon, I noticed someone who looked rather strange to me. She must have been so skinny because she had not eaten lately. Her body was rather small and I did not recall ever seeing her around these parts of the hive. She walked slowly around the idle bees outside toward the entrance of the hive. She had almost passed a warrior bee but instantly the warrior stopped her. I was far enough away that I could not hear what was being said.

I looked away for a second and admired the tall tree that neighbored our hive as several leaves fell from the branches far above. Upon turning my head back toward the strange bee I heard a loud smack! The warrior bee had just hit the skinny bee and pushed her away from the entrance. The public became frantic as some rushed in to beat up the skinny bee while others began flying away in sheer terror. I could only sit there and watch as they decimated this poor bee into the floor of the porch. Soon the beating slowed to a stop and before long the little bee was dead. I walked over to the body where the warriors were standing around.

A deep chill ran through me as I looked at the dead body. This was no skinny honeybee; it was a wasp! It was not a fellow sister bee—no: it was a brother of the wasp's nest and everyone knows what happens when a wasp is killed. The warriors looked at each other and nodded with unspoken understanding of the situation. They all swarmed around and called out for all the warriors and workers in the area around the porch to stop what they were doing and hurry to their stations. While this was happening, the dead wasp's body was precipitating a stench of a subtle scent that alarmed every wasp in the nearby area informing them that a wasp had been killed and it was time for revenge.

Masses of bees swarmed back into the hive while the ready warriors were lining up to protect the vulnerable entrance. Many shuttered to fill the gaps of empty space of the entrance as others flew in circles above to defend the hive's airspace. For a while anxiety ran through all of us because of the almost dead silence created by the incident. I hurried to take my position next to my sisters around the entrance where warriors and regular militia were standing ready for battle. I sort of nudged my way into the line and formed up with my comrades. Fear struck me as I recounted the events of a similar raid a while ago where I saw many warriors

13

and workers alike die because they lost their stingers. They were brought into the hive where I was then still working and I could remember that none of the other bees could do anything for them. They just bled-out and died moments after combat. Sometimes I would see comrades coming to the wounded bees' sides and holding them as they died traumatic, agonizing deaths.

I shook these thoughts out of my head and focused back on the situation at hand. I looked around at the line and saw that nearly all of the bees had their stingers armed. Now this is it, I thought as I brought out my stinger that had never before seen a moment of combat. On the far side of the long entrance I could see many of my colleagues coming out of the hive and into the defensive blockade. I sincerely feared for their lives as much as I feared for my own. My feeling was that no bee should die a pitiful death by the hands of savage wasps while the majority of the inner-hive oblivious to the imminent danger ahead continued to work.

Suddenly I could see the swarming bees above rush forward and away from over our heads to repel the incoming wasp attack that began with a roar of beating wings. I ducked my head behind the warrior bee in front of me as the sound got louder and louder. Before long I could hear the whizzing sound of honeybees falling and hitting the ground around the porch with a *thud*. The wasps were knocking our sisters right out of the sky! I looked up at the horror of wasps, two or three at a time, teaming up on the helpless honeybees, pulling them to the ground. They struggled against each other as each tried to sink their stingers into the other's body.

One fallen bee landed just in front of the wooden porch. The dirt was kicked up and scattered around as the bee tried desperately to repel the stinger jabs of two intimidating wasps. One of the wasps lunged its stinger into the squirming bee and pulled its abdomen out falling backwards as he started to feel the pain of removing his own stinger. The other jabbed the dying honeybee with its stinger but this time the stinger remained intact. A few of the bees in the defensive line right in front of me hurried up to the one still battle-ready wasp and surrounded him. They waited for just the right moment and swiftly they jumped onto the wasp bringing him down to the floor of the porch. Now, with no bee in front of me, I could see the full gruesome image of this wasp being ripped apart as I filled in the gap between the line. One honeybee used its strong back legs to push the wasp's triangular head down to where it was scraping against the wood of the porch as others bit off its wings and back. The once intimidating wasp was now screaming in anguish as he was literally ripped apart.

The honeybees on the frontlines recovered as I tried to take deep breaths while my heart began to pound rapidly and sink into my chest. This short skirmish was only the preface of the wasp raid which quickly became a devastating invasion. Many bees in the sky retreated back calling out to us bees on the ground.

"Make ready!" one authoritative warrior said to us, "Prepare for a countercharge!"

Countercharge? I had no idea what a countercharge was as I looked around at my comrades forming into an even tighter line formation. I did my best to go along with this plan. Then I looked up at the now visible cluster swarm of yellow-jacket wasps heading straight for us from above. After seeing brutal carnage just moments before, I was not prepared to function at the pace that these events were occurring. I shamefully considered for a moment the thought of retreating into the hive and pretending like I was doing work but this idea was hopeless and unpatriotic—I am going to fight, I promised myself.

In terror I looked up at the incoming swarm and I could count at least one hundred wasps ready to reap revenge on our hive.

"Steady....*Steady*!" The warrior instructed. In one single motion, the frontline bees leaped up into the air and instantaneously elevated to the altitude of the wasps, flying straight into them. For a split second I hesitated and saw my life flash before my eyes but I was pushed into the air by the bees behind me. My wings jolted into flight as a loud harmonious battle cry bellowed from the now airborne defensive line. With a crackle-like sound we all collided on impact with the enemy. Many of us on both sides instantly latched onto one another and fell toward the earth as others pounced on each other with stingers drawn.

I quickly avoided sudden contact with any of the wasps as they zipped around me. As the initial impact concluded, honeybees and wasps overshot each other and were forced to turn around and begin dogfighting in the air.

Many honeybees who were hit by the initial collision were thrown toward the outer wall of the hive and fell to their deaths on the Public Porch as other wasps flew into the air and fell through the heated battle. I maneuvered myself around the now spherical aerial combat zone, trying desperately to shake the wasps that were engaging me. Why on earth are they coming after me, I thought as I dipped through the swarm down to the ground beneath the swarm. Sooner or later the sounds of stinger pops rang out as many bees and wasps dropped from the battle above onto the ground like fallen angels. On the ground I found myself cowering inside of a depression in the dirt as casualties fell all around me. Luckily only dead bees and wasps fell beside me; far to my left I could see about four wasps thrashing their stingers into a dying bee that had fallen from the battle.

I looked back up at the swarm as pollen from previously working honeybees peppered the air on impact with other combatants. The feeling of pity ran through my mind and soul as many of my sisters were being brutally murdered right above me. I had to do something!

My legs lifted me from the ground and back up into the air where I shot straight up into the swarm. I yelled as loud as I could, closing my eyes and arming my stinger. I slammed through the crowd and suddenly all seemed to become silent and time seemed to slow down. I opened my eyes and looked down to find that my stinger had scraped through a passing wasp during my ascent. The wasp glided up in front of me and sprayed his blood all through the air. I could see that the air had been filled with blood, pollen, dust, legs, spent stingers, wings, and many tears—most of which were mine. The pain of ripping my stinger across the wasp's thorax started to set in as time resumed at its regular pace.

The battle was not going well for our defensive force. The wasps were decimating our militia and severely demoralizing our warriors. After much fighting in the air, nearly every honeybee in the swarm rushed back to the hive in a mad retreat. The wasps made short work of the remaining brave bees still fighting in the swarm that fought to allow a quick escape for their comrades through their own self-sacrifice. I flew close to a warrior who was somewhat leading the retreat in a disoriented manner.

"Get back! Retreat!" the warrior shouted as another warrior in the swarm quickly responded.

"No! Hold strong! No retreat! Hold the line! Forward!" The obscenely brave warrior tenaciously led a small fraction of bees out of the retreating mob and led them to their deaths by the wicked might of the wasps. Everything was happening so quickly that I could not catch a glimpse of that brave warrior's death. I flew intensely back into the hive and when I reached the temporary safety and warmth of the entrance, I felt the deep guilt and regret that I did not stand and fight with the warrior in that fatal last charge.

The herd of retreating bees ran into the hive just as a fresh force of warriors was heading out to fight. Inside of the hive I peered out toward the incoming invasion of wasps that now completely surrounded the Public Porch. I looked at the stir of bees going out of the hive and was shocked to see a close friend of mine.

"Rose!" I yelled out to her as she followed close behind a band of militia and warriors. She did not notice me in all of the confusion and I was too far from her to stop her from exiting the hive. She ran out onto the porch with an uncertain look on her face as she was anticipating her own death.

I could not let her do this. I would not standby for enough of my comrades and close friends to die for this attack to be repelled. I had to take action. Again I reversed myself back toward the porch and started for the hopeless battle outside. Rose was a dear friend of mine who stood by me when work was rough—she would do the same for me.

I squeezed my way through the masses of bees fleeing inside with their wings blown off and many had lost their stingers. Finally, after fighting the current, I was able to push through. I hit the floor of the porch outside and got to my feet, looked around. The attacking wasps were so close to me that I was almost scared to death as they brawled with other bees nearby. I instantly saw Rose flying out into the crowd and I jumped into the air. I had to stop her from fighting because if I lost her, my life as a bee would be meaningless, I thought. She flew so fast that I could not catch up to her without getting myself killed in the crossfire. Suddenly, a wasp jumped out at me with its open arms and latched onto me. I jumped and spun around, pried his arms off of me and lifted my abdomen up high. I kicked him with all of the might of my hind legs into the chaos from whence he came.

Now that I had spun around, I could not see Rose. She had disappeared into the fighting. I flew franticly through the crowd turning my head every which way, looking at the faces of the bees in combat. Rose? *Rose*?! I became oblivious to danger for a moment. It was as if I had only lost her somewhere in a regular crowd of workers. Each second that passed without a sign of her drove me to insanity. I let out a pathetic moan and continued to look in all directions for her.

For a moment I thought that I finally found her in the chaos but as I squinted through the battle, a wasp rocketed straight at me. He slammed into me and wrapped his arms and legs around me. I shook left and right helplessly. "Help!" I cried. I lifted my arms and gripped his greasy back, trying to pry him off of me.

With a shake to my right and a thrust, I was able to detach him from clasping to my body. I flew as fast as I could out of the swarm. Without looking back, I jolted out of the swarm only to hear his wings zipping right behind me in a mad chase. I flapped my wings faster and faster, flying farther and farther away from the combat zone. Quickly looking back, I could see him hunting me, panting with saliva dripping down his sharp chin. I turned my head back to my front and clenched my eyes shut, sealed with tears, frantically flying aimlessly. In a matter of seconds from the initial contact with this crazed murderer, by instinct I began to seek refuge within the large tree on the outskirts of my world. Branches with thick leaves swayed and flapped as I passed by them toward the main bark of the tree. A few leaves behind me slapped the wasp in the pursuit as he carelessly shrugged them off, illogically chasing me. I finally reached the trunk of the tree and grabbed the tough notched surface of the bark.

Running through the pockets of veiny wood, I climbed up the tree hoping to find a place to hide. For a while I climbed up with dwindling energy and a pounding heart thinking that the wasp had lost me in this wood. Eventually I stopped somewhere in the bark and squeezed myself into a notch of bark where I could remain unseen for a moment. Finally, when stopped, I could listen to the wasp's wings beat as he flew all around the tree looking for me.

I became frightened at the thought of him finding me here in this hovel with nowhere to run. The buzzing was heard all around the circumference of the tree. The wasp was circling the trunk, searching wildly for the opportunity to tear me apart. For a while I laid motionless scanning the outside with one eye open. Then all became quiet.

A tonic drop of relief soothed my blood. Was he gone, I wondered. I waited for a short while before peeking my head out of the bark over to the right— nothing but leaves. Slowly turning to my left I heard a clang and smashed my head against the wall of wood and instantly blacked out.

ENDLESS DARKNESS FILLED MY MIND. THOUGH I COULD not see or feel, I could hear a whooshing sound curving around me. The blackness slowly began to fill with color as the whooshing continued at a steady pace. Nothing could be seen; only a green blur. My head was spinning to the rate of the sound. All was slow and without feeling.

Then, all of a sudden, the tip of an antenna touched my head and the noise stopped. My eyes began to open wide and came into focus. The vast green blur became a wall of yellow that transformed into the figure of a honeybee.

"Stay still, dear, you're going to be fine," the blurred image of a honeybee said to me. The feeling in my body began to return as I realized that I was being licked on the head by this strange bee. At first I wanted to jump away, but because I had little strength, I remained still as she had instructed me. The pain started to set in on my head where I had knocked into the tree. The stranger was hemming my small concussion with her soothing tongue and mending it with her wax. "Just relax."

"W-What's going on? Where am I?" I mumbled to her.

"Just relax, friend," she responded in a pacifying voice. The mystery forced me to open my eyes and realize exactly who I was looking at. The edges around the bee became fully focused. It was the old worker bee that I had remembered seeing the previous night.

"Who are you?" I asked her with wide eyes.

"My name is Harriet," she told me in a wistful voice, "and what might your name be, young bee?"

"Shayla." I felt more comfortable around her once I knew her name. Up close I could finally appreciate the age of this old bee. All the wrinkles of a tired bee became clear. Harriet emitted the atmosphere of wisdom and great experience. For a moment I just looked at her face that was so close to mine. Then I suddenly clenched myself and felt the wound on the top of my head that Harriet had been fixing. I moved to place my hand on my head but Harriet quickly stopped me.

"No, no, let it heal, my dear." She was right, I thought, as I slowly dropped my hand down to the wood. I then looked around. The tree that offered me shelter had saved my life. I was sitting on a long horizontal branch up against the trunk that kept my back up straight against it. Harriet finished placing wax on the wound and stood up. The beautiful tree's green caught my eye and dragged my attention away toward the thick leaves swimming through the wind. Harriet had walked away for a moment and returned with a drop of honey for me. She held it to my mouth and I instinctively started to eat.

23

"Thank you," I took a breath and looked at her very confused, "what is this place?"

"Why, this is the Grand Oak," she looked at me like I was crazy, "this place is not hazardous as many of you box-dwellers seem to think." To her point, most all bees back at the hive consider this tree on the outskirts of the hive's perimeter to be extremely dangerous and filled with savages. It was only when I sat in the tree that I realized how beautiful it really was.

I took another sip of the honey and panned my eyes around Harriet to see behind her. Upon leaning over and peering out at the long horizontal branch, I could see many small grayish-brown mounds with several holes punctured through each. The mounds had no particular order along the branch; they seemed to be random in both size and placement.

"What are they?" I asked Harriet.

After shaking her head at me, she muttered, "Oh hell," and lifted me up to my feet.

I stumbled for a while until I regained my balanced and held Harriet's hand as she walked me toward the mounds. We walked past a few of the mounds that, when examined up close, seemed to resemble small bee hives of some sort. As we sauntered along the branch, several other bees poked their heads out of their small hives to look at me. Many of them just stared while others grinned. Then Harriet stepped in a pile of honey in front of one of the miniature hives and nearly stumbled.

"Oh my word, Ajani!" Harriet nudged her head inside of Ajani's hive, "What did I tell you about that?!

You best get your hive cleaned up right now, do you understand me?"

"Uh, yes'm, Miss Harriet, right away." Ajani responded in sheer fear and embarrassment. Harriet backed out of her hive and stepped around the spilled honey back over to me. Her authority around this tree became clear to me. We continued our walk along the wide branch passing these makeshift hives left and right. I could not wait any longer. I had to start asking questions.

"Well what was that back there?" I exclaimed.

"That's just this bee Ajani, she came here all the way from a place called Florida to the south. She's what some bees around here call a 'killer bee.' She can be a real pain sometimes because she lives recklessly, but she does a hell of a job in combat."

"Yeah, but what was she living in?" I tried to get an answer to this mystery. She looked over at me while we were walking and then looked back forward.

"I am not sure that you know what freedom is all about here in the Grand Oak," she slowed to a stop and looked at me, "this is how bees are supposed to live, in harmony with the tree. You have much to learn, Shayla."

All of this talk about freedom made me think for a moment that I was among savages, but it was the beauty of the tree that kept me from flying away. What did she mean by *real* freedom, I wondered. She motioned for us to continue walking as she continued to explain.

"Every bee here is here by their own will, every bee here supports the other, every creature here knows how

25

to live with the Grand Oak, don't you see?" I tried to understand what she was talking about but I could do nothing but walk and look around flipping a million questions through my mind. Then she passively said to me, "I did not have to save you from that wasp, you know." And then I gasped loudly.

"Oh no! The hive!" Memories of how I got here in the first place began to reappear in my head. "I need to go." I told Harriet.

"That box that you call a hive is in shambles right now. The only safe place out here is in the Grand Oak."

"Shut up!" I yelled at her looking around restlessly with my hand on my wound.

"If you don't believe me I implore you to see for yourself." I jumped into flight and dropped out of the tree and headed straight for the hive while Harriet just stood there watching me.

I flew low to the ground and away from the tree toward the hive. My flapping became slower as I saw the bodies of the dead lying all over the dirt and in the grass. They all appeared as the result of horrific carnage leaving anguished poses from violent deaths. Bees I knew and bees I never knew.

As I neared the hive I suddenly stopped in a patch of grass observing the state of the hive. There were honeybees and wasps alike wandering the fields around the hive. Some looking for the way home while others walked without life. Those wasps that were still relatively intact ran fatigued out of the hive with a wealth of stolen honey and honeycombs. They ran as fast as

26

they could, the ones that were able to get away that is, from the pursuit of honeybees that had just lost their fortunes and hard work.

I eventually started walking toward the hive entrance where the dead were stacked high. They had been amassing the dead in piles around the entrance as blockades against further attacks. Inside of the hive all was in chaos. Bees and warriors were crying out in agony over their wounds and dying while others were begging for the return of their stolen honey. There were also a few silent warrior bees that stood by, waiting for the wounded to die to stack them in the piles outside. Although the attack was ultimately repelled, the hive suffered the most from the assault and our bees managed to only cut down a fraction of the beepower of the enemy.

Many bees comforted the dying bees as they passed on. A very delicate bee was with another sister on the floor of the hive. I could not tell who it was so I walked closer. It was Charlie talking calmly to dying Rose. I gasped and Charlie noticed me.

"...Welcome home, Shayla," she said in an increasingly angered tone, "I see you have a wound on your head, did you get that from running like a coward from the battlefield?" She now became terribly maddened by my presence there, especially in front of Rose.

"Charlie, I did my best, I couldn't find Rose in the air." My eyes welled up, "I'm sorry Rose," said I looking down at her. Rose was lying flat on the ground with her eyes closed, too hurt to speak or even know what was going on. Charlie stood up and left her for a second.

"You get out of here, Shayla." She said directly into my face. I hesitated for a moment and realized that if I did not leave she would kill me right there on the spot. Fearfully, I backed up but still remained focused on her deep black eyes. I looked down at Rose for the last time and then back at Charlie.

"I'm sorry." My words meant nothing, because I was a coward. On my way out of the hive other bees who noticed my encounter with Charlie hollered at me.

"Traitor! Deserter! Coward!" All of these things filled my heart with lasting pain and guilt. I felt my whole colony and compatriots damning me to hell. Finally I realized that this hive could never again be my home.

It was time for me to leave. I had nothing to take with me, no one to say goodbye to, just regret and sorrow is all I took. I managed to make my way out of the hive without looking back or responding to the ridicule. However, I could hear an almost mob-like crowd following behind me shooting hateful words into my ears. "Yeah, just keep walking, coward!" Walking out from the hive I felt the wood of the Public Porch once more and began to walk on the bloodstained dirt. I looked back for a second and saw the crowd of bees looking at me standing on the porch.

"I always knew you were nothing but a selfish coward, Shayla!" someone yelled to me. "Never come back, you—ecgghh echhh." The bees started to cough and wheeze. Many of them moved back into the hive as a white haze of smoke fell down upon the hive. They stopped paying attention to me and went back to their business. I turned away and looked up at the tall oak tree. Harriet was right, I thought, there really was no place for me here anymore.

Reluctantly, I knew that the only place I could go now was back to the Grand Oak and apologize to Harriet for my ingratitude toward her hospitality. The sun was setting on this day of bloodshed, and now the only viable home offered to me was to be the oak tree among the savages. Flying slowly up to the Grand Oak I thought deeply about the kind of alterations I would have to make in my life to adapt to this savage but beautifully lush environment. As the sun set, the dark green leaves of the tree blackened to the night while the tree wept in the cold wind over the dead.

Harriet was sitting on the large branch where I had left her looking down at me as I slowly approached. I reached her and sat beside her looking out to the distance where the moon was rising over the silent night. We sat there without words for a while. After a long breath, I broke the peaceful silence.

"I'm sorry, Miss Harriet." She turned to me but did not respond. I looked back at her and opened up, "Thank you for saving me before." She was about to respond but I added to my apology statement, "And you were right about that hive down there, it's totally ruined."

"It was built to be ruined, Shayla." This profound response made me look at her with perplexity. "That hive down there is nothing but a prison. It was built to keep you enslaved and its tyranny has been growing for years."

"I don't understand. How do you know this?"

"You, Shayla, were born here like most all other bees down in those hives. I was one of the first to actually be *brought* here to this place." She looked out at the moon and continued to tell her story. "The difference between you and I is that I was born in freedom and taken into slavery while you were born in slavery and will soon know true freedom."

"How were you taken here, Harriet?"

"I was first captured in the wild by the devils and pushed into a compressed bin with no hope of escape. There were hundreds of bees there all trying to look for a way out but none succeeded as all of us were taken here to this place. You see, they brought us here to place us in those boxes that you call hives down there and exploit us for all of our honey and energy. I knew how my life was going to end down there when they brought us here, so when they opened the bin to let us into the hive, I flew as fast as I could away from the boxes and sought shelter. This tree became my home, for it stands as the only *real* protection in this area. I love the Grand Oak and will always call it my home."

"But there are other bees living here too, how did they get here?"

"Some of the bees here were always here while some others escaped here as I did back in those days of construction." She realized nearly every word she spoke needed to be explained to me, and so she let out a small sigh. "This 'hive' that you were born in is just one of many artificially made box-hives that sit on this ground called the Oersted Farm. Through the years all the members of the Grand Oak have lived with relative prosperity while we watch you box-dwellers down there. We occasionally scavenge for nectar like all other bees but do not have to give up most of it to that devil down there who is your keeper."

"Who do you mean?"

"You bees make all this excess honey, working tire-lessly day after day and don't even know where it all goes! There is a monster down there that is stealing masses of honey from your hives and leaving only a fraction for your colony to eat. Here, the Grand Oak is our master who wishes for us to live free, unlike that devil beekeeper."

"Well if this is all true, then why haven't I ever seen the beekeeper?" I asked Harriet.

"You don't see him because he sprays that smoke all over you. When he comes to steal your honey, he peppers your entire hive with smoke that clouds your colony's consciousness. That is why you continue to work and do not think!"

It all was gradually becoming clear to me. I guess I never thought about where the honey goes once we finish producing it. Sitting in the Grand Oak gave me a harmonious feeling of security even in the dark of night. The inhabitants of the Grand Oak must not be affected by the smoke sprayed down below, I thought.

"But wait, Harriet, does the Grand Oak have a queen?"

31

"The Grand Oak requires no such thing," I was shocked at the idea of no queen and seemingly no royalty, "but we do have a leader—a leader that is in fact part of the Grand Oak." She could read my thoughts effortlessly, "I could take you to him if you wish."

"Yes ma'am, I'd love to see your leader." She scanned my face and stood up with me. Without any further ado, we were on our way to meet this leader in the midst of the night. Harriet continued to explain terminology and a few details about their reasons for being here which I did not understand because I still lacked the capacity to comprehend what she meant. As it turned out, we began to walk on the same path where we had first met; I could perceive that Harriet wanted to show me to him when we first met, but the course of events chose otherwise.

All was quiet along the straight branch. Those that slept napped comfortably in their modest hives. As we neared to the tip of the branch I could start to see a round bowl-like coagulation of twigs seated firmly at the end of the branch. The closer we got to the tip, the clearer the quiet conversations there became. Soon we were finally at the mass of twigs and peeked into it as the moonlight shot down on the bees inside.

Harriet and I looked down into the case of twigs and saw twelve bees sitting around a wide leaf that had engraved on it some sort of diagram of the land. Their conversations were intense and their tongues spoke with eloquence and learned tones. They were not savages as many from down below wanted to believe. I did not want to disturb them as they seemed to be working

32

diligently on some sort of plan. Harriet leaned over to me and began to whisper.

"Say your name—say it proudly."

"What?" I was confused. Then suddenly a low voice bellowed out from the darkness.

"Who have you brought me tonight, Harriet?" I was shocked at the resonance of this voice, and I was speechless for a moment until Harriet nudged me in the back.

"Uh, Shayla! From the Meridian Hive." My voice was weak and my lack of confidence or understanding drew much attention. The twelve bees below stopped their business for a second and looked up at me. I looked at Harriet who was smiling delightfully.

"Any prison that is propped up to tyrannize its bees earns no recognition from me. But your name is true and without depravity. Shayla you are, and Shayla you will be." Suddenly, a large dark figure emerged out of the darkness beyond the twigs stepping into the foreground. Then the moonlight shined upon the figure and I looked up at the unbelievably large creature.

"I am Meadowlark, and this tree is my home. It is as much *my* home as it is *yours*." He stood high above all of us, with a golden yellow vest of feathers, spotted white wings, and a black scarf of plumage around his neck. His body was thick and strong with a sharp beak and disproportionately skinny brown legs. I looked stunned at him for a while until Harriet intervened in my euphoric encounter with Meadowlark.

"Shayla here went through a lot today; perhaps it would be alright if she reclines here with us in the nest tonight?"

"We would be privileged to have her in our company," Meadowlark responded courteously. I looked back at Harriet to see if I had the permission to sit. She nodded, and we all sat around the wide leaf at the base of the nest. The conversation among the other bees began to pick up again. Harriet and I sat close behind the circle of bees while Meadowlark sat slightly displaced from the group, only listening to the discussion without interjecting.

"Now, as you can see, the pickup zone is here at the end of the wide path leading to the devil's chamber." One of the bees pointed at the leaf and was explaining something. I looked down where he was pointing and tried to understand the markings. Though I had no comprehension, I was intrigued by their sophistication and their discussion. "We will send two scouts by dawn to the end of the bush line here where the pickup-demon awaits Oersted and complete the sketch of this map by sunset."

"Splendid, Councilbee Rosa, it appears that because of all of our hard work in this somewhat menial endeavor, we will soon have an idea of what we are up against—let us all be proud—Oak be praised!"

"*Oak be praised*," they all responded. Then there was a small silence and I looked over at Meadowlark who spoke in conclusion of the meeting.

"Let this act of surveying lead us one step closer to achieving our goals of restoring freedom to this land.

Go now, my sisters, to rest, for by tomorrow night this map will be whole, and from there our plans will be realized." All the twelve bees stood up, rolled the map into a long scroll and together carried it out of the nest across the Long Branch into the darkness. Harriet got up and vanished with them while I sat there thinking and shivering slightly from the cold. Meadowlark stepped to my left, curled his large wing around me and sat. I had never felt so comfortable around a leader before in my life, though this leader appeared to be the size of a monster, his presence was lovely and grand. I looked up at him while he warmed me with his spotted white feathers and yellow breast.

"My condolences..." He said to me in a solemn voice, "no colony deserved what your hive received today. I pray for your sisters down there, Shayla. We watch you from up here each day of our lives—hoping that one morning we will be able to assist you all. But the Grand Oak has prevented us from intervention up until now, after that attack, we cannot wait any longer."

"I appreciate your words sir, but I am afraid I can see no remedy for my hive. I see no hope for my fellow sisters. I am unable to even return because they believe I am a coward and a traitor." I tilted my head down somberly and sulked. Meadowlark embraced me.

"Shayla, what you are experiencing now is only the first stage of your awakening. When you sleep in the night and lie there calm and undisturbed, the morning will come without any formal announcement, shine light beams straight into your eyes, and at first, you will abhor the sun, and wish for the moment that you were

35

still in darkness. But the sun will bring you warmth, vision, and hope, just as this tree and these bees give me hope." Meadowlark raised my spirits as I looked up at him right above my head. "You may not yet perceive it, but the Grand Oak has brought you here for a reason. Of all those bees down there, the suffering and the content, the warriors and the workers, you were sent here to learn something. One day you will return to your hive and there they will hail you as their hero, all in the name of what you will bring them."

"What could *I* bring them?"

"Freedom." Meadowlark was silent for a moment and allowed the word to bounce through my mind. "You will be able to bring it to them once you are able to perceive it."

"I'm trying but I just—I can't!" I became very irritated and growled with frustration that I could not comprehend this concept. I just could not understand what he meant. I was trying so hard.

"Relax my friend, we will teach you and in time you will see." I took a deep breath and again considered myself living among these strange creatures in this strange tree—everything was just so different—my mind simply could not comprehend their lifestyle or their knowledge which I admired. Meadowlark held me tightly as the wind began to howl through the leaves.

"Meadowlark…why are you not like us bees?" He could see that I was searching for the right words. "I mean, you have the same colors as us, black and yellow, but you are tall, you are strong, and you are a bird."

"I am no different than any of you. We all originated from this tree, and this is our home, you see. The way that we have all arrived at this place and at this time may be different but our home has always been, and will always be, the tree. The day I first opened my eyes, I was perched in this very nest where we sit. I was totally dependent on my parents who would bring me food from nearby, never too far from the Grand Oak though. But one day when I was very young, I heard the loud blasts of the devils' weapons. My head jolted up and I could hear hot metal flying through the air and chipping branches off this tree. There were two young devils below, hollering and laughing like savages, shooting their metal erratically. I looked around and all of a sudden I saw my mother and father squawking and flapping their wings from the nearby branches. They quickly hopped right in front of the nest together and stood with their wings out wide. Without aim or motive, those young devils below shot my parents and they fell straight to the ground. Though many of the shots from the devils' tools pierced the Oak's skin, I remained unharmed in the nest that my mother and father had built me. From then on I would never be the same. My hate for the devils would continue till my end." Meadowlark took a breath and then continued. "As a young chick without parents, I was raised by the Grand Oak, you see. The tree would show me where to find food and how to fly between branches. In those days there used to be hundreds of oak trees across this land that gave me protection and comfort among them. But over the years they were cut down to clear the land for the devil's work. They had cut down nearly all of the trees around this one, but for some reason they did not seem to topple the Grand Oak." Meadowlark gave a short smile and looked out past the tree.

"That's horrible." I could almost feel the pain of the tragic loss of his parents. "But then why do you stay here?"

"I stay because I happen to know that those two boy-devils that killed my parents still lurk in this land, and the one that pulled the trigger I know to be Oersted, the king of all evil." He lifted his left wing and pointed it out forward past the nest. "At this moment you are not able to perceive it, but there is something called a 'house' over yonder near the box-hives that contains the Oersted devil himself…and his family." My imagination ran wild. Through Meadowlark's explanation, the outline of Oersted was drawn in my mind and all I could see was a tall monster who ate birds and bees alike—a demon, as Meadowlark described. Then I tried to imagine his family but could not easily perceive their ills. Then Meadowlark opened up his heart with its deepest aspirations. "Oersted will be mine, and his blood will quench my thirst and the thirst of the Grand Oak." Meadowlark became very serious and determined to instill this ambition in my mind as solid as it was in his. He looked over at me and we both stared into each other's eyes. It appeared, through his eyes, that his entire life's purpose was to kill Oersted and to skewer his severed head to the highest branch on the Grand Oak.

Without knowing how to respond, I simply nodded to Meadowlark and inched closer to him, embracing him tightly. He did not speak another word that night. We just sat there listening to the cold wind pass by our ears. I soon felt discourteous at overstaying my welcome with Meadowlark. By this notion, I stood up and thanked Meadowlark kindly and stepped out of the nest. As I walked along the Long Branch, Meadowlark began to chirp at the moon. What a spirit resides in that bird, I thought to myself walking, wishing that I could one day emanate his greatness.

Most of the modest hives were dark and held many sleeping bees. I noticed one of the hives gleaming with the light from the golden honey inside shining out of the portholes. It was Harriet awaiting my arrival. I neared the hive and stepped in. Harriet had prepared a cradle for me to sleep in. She restfully motioned for me to come in and recline in the cradle that she had set out for me. I thanked her gratefully and began to rest in the soft crib made from natural wax and leaves. When I began to relax, I looked over at Harriet who was closing the lights of the honey and retiring to her cradle as well. I opened my mouth to say thank you, but before a word was even spoken, she smiled at me and drifted right to sleep. Soon, I would follow her in into my dreams. "Thank you" I whispered softly to her and then fell asleep.

THE MORNING CAME WITHOUT WARNING. THE LIGHT FROM the sun leaped into the hive and pierced my eyes with absolute brilliance. I quickly shut them and faced down to avoid the light but realized that I truly could not escape. I raised my head out of the cradle and lifted myself out. The morning looked beautiful outside from the comfort of the hive. I licked my skin into a presentable stature and exited the hive.

The sky was a bluish grey with no clouds. The air was warm and fresh, radiating from the Grand Oak. I looked down at the box-hives below and saw that the Meridian Hive, my former home, was still in a dire state of distress as honeybees swarmed around it in mass chaos. The other box-hives remained relatively calm and unsympathetic toward the Meridian Hive, offering no help or assistance to my forsaken sisters. I then became distracted by the moderate bustle along the Long Branch in the Grand Oak. Bees were passing by, organizing outside some hives and working inside others. *A bee is always busy*, I thought.

Today, I would begin my journey into the world of *freedom*, as Meadowlark called it. I felt the need to get my hands dirty and work to become a part of this whole operation here. Amongst the hustle and bustle of the tree, I could not spot Harriet in the various crowds. It occurred to me that I needed to initiate my involvement *by myself* this time. I felt that Harriet would want me to show how much I believed in this freedom thing myself to all of the other bees before I could be accepted by them.

I walked aimlessly around swinging my arms by my side looking at all of the passing bees. Many of them looked at me with a sort of instant acceptance because it appeared that they had found out that Meadowlark had accepted me. Some bees looked at me suspiciously and did not quite believe that I belonged here yet—I was as unsure as they were about my presence here. Trying to be instantaneous I began walking with a group of bees that were strolling and talking together. I followed quietly behind them trying to blend in before one of them noticed me.

"Well look who it is, the new-bee!" I anticipated the ridicule but was surprised when one of the other bees latched her arm around my shoulders. "It's about time we meet a new face around here. What's your name?"

"My name's Shayla," I said and smiled to them as they smiled back at me.

"Well my name is Elizabeth, that's Emily, and this is Anne. We like to think of ourselves as our own sisterhood." They began to laugh and look at me. I began to laugh with them and walked at their pace.

"That's swell. So where are you girls headed right now?" I tried to fit in with them and hopefully join them on their affairs of the day. They began to laugh again. Anne leaned over to me and raised her finger.

"Well right now, we are just strolling and enjoying our freedom." Anne smiled at me while I felt slightly excluded because I did not know what she meant. "But we are going to the assembly at the High Branch in a little while. You can join us if you'd like—every bee we know is going to be there." We walked peacefully across the branches and stopped for a while to look at the rising sun and the pretty flowers in bushes below. At the sight of the flowers I jumped and almost took off flying before Emily stopped me.

"Woah, what's going on, Shayla?!"

"Marigolds! We need to get nectar!" I was babbling and jumping around, twisting my wings to be ready for flight.

"Calm down Shayla, there is no need to get more nectar, we have enough honey stored in this tree to last us nearly two winters." Emily's words tried to calm me down. I realized that I was having trouble adjusting to the lifestyle of the Grand Oak bees. I thought back to what Harriet told me about the devil taking a large portion of honey from the box-hive that I lived in before. Here in this tree, the devil would not be able to take any honey away, so the bees here must not have to work as hard to fill their combs. I finally stopped frantically flapping my wings and landed my feet back on the bark.

"Oh, I'm sorry, how embarrassing," I blushed. "So you bees don't harvest every flower you see when they come into your field of view?" The three looked at me like I was mad.

"No, we'd much rather appreciate their beauty and only harvest the nectar if need be." This all was common sense to them but absolute insanity to my box-hive-bred mind. I then understood what she was saying and looked down again at the marigolds trying to refrain from the lustful appetite for their nectar. Their frilled petals of yellow reminded me of Meadowlark's feather breast that kept me warm during the night, before *and* after the encounter with him. The gentle morning air allowed the flowers to dance and soak up the hot glory of the sun. The four of us sat and watched them as we lost track of the time. After an unperceivable amount of minutes passed, Elizabeth sprung up from her sitting position and looked at all of us as we slowly looked at her, reluctantly breaking our focus from the mesmerizing marigolds.

"Girls, the assembly!" She leaped into the air fluttering her wings as each of us followed her into flight. Before long, we were soaring through the Grand Oak, dodging branches and leaves on our way to the top. In a matter of moments we came within ear's distance of the assembly meeting where nearly one hundred bees were sitting tightly next to each other. We slowed our flapping to lessen the amount of noise we were creating that might disturb the meeting. We crept into the crowd of bees, unnoticed because of the speech that was in progress during our dramatic entry. Soon we found a place where all four of us could stand together on the High Branch and look up at the speaker standing near the top of the incline who had the attention of the entire crowd.

"Oak brings us light, Oak brings us sight, Oak gives us strength across branches length, grant us freedom and we shall fight, for we will prepare day and night." The assembly appeared to be opened by some sort of spontaneous prayer given by the speaker. "Oak be praised!" The bee bellowed to the audience as the crowd shouted the words back at her. "Today, we assemble to discuss the status of our endeavors. It has been brought to my attention that you bees have been anxious to know what Meadowlark thinks about the recent wasp raid at the Meridian Hive." The whole crowd went crazy and cried for information on Meadowlark's opinion of the attack. The speaker calmed them down and began to tell us all. "Meadowlark feels that this attack has given us the perfect opportunity to rally the still imprisoned bees down below to our cause! He believes that we must move quickly now and show them what freedom is all about!" The speaker's words threw the audience into huge applause and lasting joy throughout the assembly.

"What are we to do?!" some bee cried out to the speaker while others around her were eager to know how exactly the bees of the Grand Oak would do this.

"In this time of distress for the Meridian Hive, we will help them rebuild themselves and show them how they can be free as we are with the Grand Oak. They will see that our lifestyle is superior to slavery and will join our cause to free all the bees of this wretched farm!" While much of the crowd cheered in agreement with the speaker, I could not help but think how terribly difficult it would be to rebuild the crumbling hive. Those bees down there are probably killing each other over the last of their honeycombs and the warriors must be taking over all aspects of the hive's functions. It became my theory that the Meridian Hive would inevitably become unsustainable and if the bees were to survive, they would need sustenance and adequate honey comparable to that of the hives in the Grand Oak. While I thought these things, I looked up past the speaker and past the tip of the High Branch and saw the leaves suddenly open up. It was Meadowlark descending from the canopy of the Grand Oak, swooping down behind the speaker. Everyone gasped and cheered for Meadowlark in almost total disregard of the speaker whose name was not yet known to me.

"Indeed we must show the prisoners the way of freedom, but we must not and *cannot* do so by rebuilding the facilities that have kept them enslaved—with the Grand Oak as our guide and foundation, we must first tear down the evils of Oersted before we will be able to rebuild the hives the way they were supposed to be—as one with the Oak!" The entire crowd listened to Meadowlark intensely and whispered little. Then the speaker turned to Meadowlark and respectfully responded.

"Meadowlark sir, then what are the bees from the Meridian Hive to do if we do not rebuild it for them?"

"They will be forced to abandon it, for its very wooden structure inhibits them from becoming like us. We cannot simply seek remedy for them and expect them to join us if they are able to live in a state of pretentious prosperity. They must know and feel the pain, suffering, and lack of sympathy from the Oersted devil to see the truth!" Meadowlark's words surpassed any contributions the speaker or any other bee could have made at the assembly that morning. "We will spark an absolute revolution on this land that cannot stop, cannot wander for even a moment. Our actions must be swift, deadly, and strategic if we are to succeed. There is no compromise with Oersted! We cannot live alongside the evils below us while we rejoice in freedom above—this inequality is not desired by the Grand Oak. We are guilty of allowing our fellow creatures to suffer unduly by the devil's tyranny while we enjoy the freedom that is available to *all* creatures, not just us. Though we have fought hard for our freedom and have made great sacrifices to get here, we are no better than any other creatures that have not yet been chosen by the Grand Oak." Meadowlark's language of equality and total revolution slightly altered the perspective of the crowd. It became clear that the coexistence between the Grand Oak and the Oersted Farm was simply unstable and unnatural—it was to be one or the other with no exceptions.

Many of the bees had been accustomed to the coexistence of the farm and the tree for years apparently. Ever since I could remember in my days in the Meridian Hive there was talk about the savages that lived in the tall tree and how they would live as a small band of outcasts beside the so-called civilized bees that we were. With Meadowlark's expression, the state of mind had shifted and no longer would the Grand Oak seek to be a home for *some* but truly a home for *all*.

"Forgive me for my intrusion; I yield the floor." Meadowlark then stood behind the speaker motionless with his wings folded around himself. For a moment, the speaker did not know how to continue the assembly after Meadowlark's address. But soon the speaker gathered his thoughts and spoke.

"Is an absolute revolution what you desire, my sisters?!" The audience roared in affirmation to the speaker and Meadowlark. The speaker energetically riled them up further by encouraging them to scream louder so that all the box-hives below could hear. "Then an absolute revolution it will be!" Most all of the bees applauded while some were in agreement but wary about the cost involved in accomplishing the task. The girls and I looked at each other to see how each of us was taking this. Anne, Emily, and Elizabeth were cheering and jumping up-and-down in excitement. I could not help but join them.

We jumped as part of the ocean of bees and contributed to the deafeningly loud cheering. The excitement ran through me like never before. For once in my life I actually felt like I was part of a family with a common goal in mind. Soon, the bees began to calm down and the assembly resumed.

"As you are well aware, our two brave scouts assisted by the Council will be returning by nightfall with the completed schematics of the entire farm as well as the inside of the devil's lair. Note that this was no easy task and the Council should be justly applauded and compensated for their efforts." A few bees in the crowd whispered among themselves, mostly about how shocked they were at the fact that the scouts were able to infiltrate the devil's lair and escape with their lives. The speaker looked for a moment back at Meadowlark who was nodding his head for him to continue. "With this map completed we will be able to pinpoint the necessary objectives that need to be neutralized in order to blaze a path for our mission. However, these targets cannot be successfully taken without the beepower of the entire farm. Our modest battalion of bees in the Grand Oak lacks the numbers that we require to achieve our aims, so it is absolutely necessary that we rally each of the five box-hives to our cause before we are able to strike."

One bee stood up out of the crowd and yelled her question to the speaker. "How shall we rally them if they believe we are savages?!" Her question was valid and I equally desired an answer to this. "To assemble them we will require their recognition," she continued. Suddenly my heart started to pound. Meadowlark unfolded his wings and stepped forward next to the speaker. All the focus of the assembly shifted to him as he began to address the question.

"Who better to assist us in the task than one of their own!" The whole audience looked around and then was guided by Meadowlark's outstretched wing pointed directly at me from afar. "A new sister has joined us among the Grand Oak. She has been chosen by the Oak to be free from the box-hive that begot her in slavery. Let her set the example for the rest of the slaves below, for she has shown courage and strength by her arrival!" Then, after informing the crowd, Meadowlark looked deeply into my eyes. "Your strength and knowledge is now required, young Shayla. Will you rally with us and help awaken the slaves below?" Addressing me personally, Meadowlark forced me into total shock and embarrassment from the intense attention of the crowd. With my heart beating out of my chest and everyone staring at me, I stood up.

"...Yes I will!" Emotional and nervous, I received a welcoming and encouraging applause from the bees and from Meadowlark. The bees and my three young friends called for me to go on. Though I was nervous and shaky, I still managed to speak with a strange confidence in my words, as if the Grand Oak was speaking through me. "I will gladly serve, and will gladly fight in the name of the Grand Oak!" Though I was not completely socially accepted among them, I attempted to use their collective phrase; "Oak be praised!" They all responded immediately and demonstrated their true acceptance of me; *Oak be praised.* Meadowlark smiled at me and spoke happily.

"My sisters, this is the face of our revolution. This is the face of the new-bee; awoken from bondage and drawn to the cause of liberty!" The cheering bees to my side crowded around me and shook me with love and affection. The entire audience was energized by my simple presence and cherished the moment as I did. I was shaken and nervous like a newborn larva. The attention was unstoppable and nearly disorienting. Luckily, Meadowlark shifted the attention back to the stage of the High Branch and hushed the audience. The speaker kept looking at me and spoke verily.

"We welcome you, Shayla, with the Grand Oak as our witness. Let us conclude this assembly with a closing statement from our beloved Meadowlark, if he would please." The speaker looked over at Meadowlark, stepped backwards and allowed him to take the floor. Meadowlark spread his wings out wide and then tucked them back to his sides.

"It seems that all that needed to be said has been said here and now. We must prepare the divisions of sisters into our glorious formations to be ready for battle with the enemy as well as for peace with our sisters below. You are all dismissed." The crowd of bees, eager for action, leaped into the air and flew in all directions while the cacophony of wing flapping muddled the side-conversations of the few still seated bees. The recognition and praise from the bees next to me continued for a while as they lifted me up and carried me off of the High Branch and down the tree trunk. Smiling, I looked down to see that the three girls were indeed holding me up.

"Where are we going?" I asked with my joyous but trembling voice.

"To the barracks at the base of the Oak! There is a lot you need to learn, sister!" Elizabeth spoke to me with the most accepting and loving voice I had ever heard. As we paraded down the trunk, some of the bees scattered away and rushed to their obligations. Elizabeth, Anne, Emily, and I continued to walk further down the tree while some other bees followed close behind. Soon we reached the base of the tree and hopped down to the thick roots that were sticking out of the ground where the Grand Oak connected to the earth. The girls put me down and brushed me off.

"Well, here we are."

Looking toward the bottom of the Grand Oak we could see a small pocket in the root structure that was dark and open like a tunnel into the depths of the ground below the tree. Several bees before us rushed inside and disappeared into its blackness. The four of us crawled down to the mossy green floor and walked into the hole. Inside we were covered in darkness as noise from below echoed through the tunnel to the outside.

I stepped closer to Anne and held her hand as we descended into the dark abyss. We crawled down to the deepest level of the chasm and finally saw light glistening on the dirt. We came to the entrance of a lit room and stepped inside into the golden light.

It was a large, flat area where just enough dirt had been cleared away for the floor to be sturdy but also riddled with thin grey roots sticking up out of it. The corners of the room were lit with walls of honey that shined a caramel light all around. Passing by were bees getting ready for exercise and training of some sort. Soon the room filled up with bees and we all naturally ordered ourselves into rows of five spread out across the entirety of the area. Within moments the other bees including my young friends began to stretch and flex their muscles on the floor. They all committed to countless push-ups on the floor while I slowly followed behind them.

My panting was so loud that it nearly became a disturbance to the other bees. Though I would have collapsed of fatigue, the energy attained from the infinite attention I received earlier pushed me to continue the work-out until it was through. Just as the group evenly concluded the exercise, one of them in the formation yelled "HUH!" and all the bees stood up to start the next exercise.

We all lined up against one of the dirt walls in the room. The lead bee who was embedded among us cried again "Huh!" and we began crawling quickly around the whole circumference of the room at an immense speed.

The running began with great haste as I tried to keep up with all of them. Before long, a chant was initiated by the group that's resonance circled the room just as we did.

"O, A, K, Oak! O, A, K, Oak!" We all began to chant this cadence with a combined emphasis on the impact of the word '*Oak*'. The very act of chanting kept me from collapsing as the bees behind me persistently pushed me to continue.

O, A, K, Oak! There appeared to be no end to the chanting or the running. I could feel my body beginning to weaken at the strain. Finally, we completed our constant cycle of running around the circle and ran out of the room back into the darkness. We huffed our chant through the echoing hallway and hurried up a ramp of roots into another room.

Inside this room there were less lights and the area was longer rather than wide like the previous room. Along one side of the room were poles of wax wrapped in fallen leaves. As we passed by each of them we turned to them and jabbed them with our abdomens where our stingers would be if armed. At every pole of wax we would thrust our unarmed stingers in and hear a satisfying *crunch* inside. We would continue this stepping and jabbing until the last bee had finished the line.

At the other end of the long room we departed back into the darkness where I again followed close behind the bees in front of me for guidance through the maze of dark interconnected tunnels. We made a last push, exhausting all of our strength, and finally made it out of the hole and back to the surface where the thick roots of the Grand Oak touched the ground.

"Atten...HUT!" With a loud *stomp*, our line came to a tight halt and we all faced sideways, shoulder to shoulder. The whole time I was constantly one step behind the other bees who presumably had been conducting these exercises for a very long time. But now that we were stopped for a moment, I was able to catch my breath and synchronize with the pace of the other bees. Then suddenly one of the bees ordered us to arm our stingers.

I extended my stinger painfully out of my abdomen as the others armed their stingers swiftly. With another "Huh!" we all began stabbing the air in front of us and behind us with our razor-sharp stingers. The idea of this exercise was not to practice using your stinger against an opponent but rather to use it safely around your fellow comrades in battle without cutting them as you move between targets. I moved at a much slower speed at this time and took extra care not to cut my fellow bee and had to focus on learning the basic techniques like these if I was ever to be as confident in battle as they were.

As we progressed, we practiced many variations of stinger-to-stinger combat and how to move as one unit rather than as individuals that would flee if proper support was not provided by the unity of the group. We trained and trained as the sun above our heads drifted through the sky as the time passed. Even though I was tired, I was proud to be active among the bees and not motionless as I would be if I did not stumble upon these three accepting young bees who became my companions.

The training began to wind down. I began to wonder what Harriet was doing at the moment. She was a very important bee around the Grand Oak, after all, so I would not be surprised to know that she was quite occupied at the moment—*a bee is always busy*.

After a gradual decline in pace, the training exercises were over and I dropped to the ground fatigued. A few bees wandered off back up the trunk of the tree while I sat there letting out huge sighs. My muscles were beating over the hard work and burned inside of my body. I looked at the rest of the bees that were standing around, wiping sweat off of their faces. Elizabeth approached me and lifted me up to my feet.

"Well, what did you think?" She asked me while I nearly fell backwards from the dizziness.

"I think you were right, Elizabeth. I do have a lot to learn." I smiled at her and she hugged me. My body was so overworked that I became quite famished and looked at Elizabeth with a strange sort of expression. "Do you think we could get some honey to eat?" Elizabeth laughed and patted me on the shoulder.

"I thought you'd never ask, because that's exactly where we're headed next." Elizabeth kept her arm around my shoulder while she gathered the other two girls who were chatting quietly. Soon we were all walking happily back up the tree headed for the Long Branch. Though I was openly exhausted, the girls appeared nearly unaffected by the rigorous training. Nonetheless, we were all starving.

We reached the intersection of the trunk and the Long Branch and stepped on. The entire Long Branch was bustling with traffic as it always did. Many bees were passing around small leaf pamphlets that some read in groups while others read on-the-go. I wondered what they were.

"Hey girls, what are those leaves for?"

"Oh, that's the *Oak Leaf*, it's pretty good." As we passed by, some of the reading bees looked over at me specifically and then down at the leaf and then back at me again. "And your name is probably all over it, Shayla." How flattering, I thought. But I still wondered what its contents were exactly.

"I think I am going to grab one." Curiously I walked over to a stack of the pamphlets and took one off of the pile.

"Help yourself, there is no shortage here." The pages were green with serrated marks all over. As I opened the *Oak Leaf*, I realized that the inscriptions on it were in a language that I could not understand. Then Emily pointed to one mark on the leaf.

"See, right here; *'Shayla'*." I studied the leaf for a good few moments and could not comprehend the words. I looked up at Emily and the rest of the girls.

"What?" The girls giggled at my confusion. "Who am I kidding, I can't read this." Laughing, I placed the leaf back on the pile and continued walking and giggling with the girls. We then remembered how famished we were and all agreed that it was time for us to get a bit of honey to eat.

The girls and I came to a large hive where honey was being served to everyone at no expense at all. The Dining Hall was filled with bees laughing and talking together around piles of fresh golden honey. Many were reading the *Oak Leaf* in one hand and gracefully sipping honey from the other. The room had a joyous atmosphere with tranquil feasting happening all around. Elizabeth got us all onto the line of bees taking honey from the enormous honeycomb that was clean and without imperfections seated at the middle of the Dining Hall. We dipped our hands into the combs and pulled out a handful of honey on top of the wax that held the combs together. The girls and I inverted the honey to being on top of the wax that served as a convenient plate.

Looking around for a place to sit, we wandered over to one corner of the Dining Hall and found a spot. We sat down and began eating the honey. It was pleasantly delicious and quite refreshing. We sat in a circle together calmly eating and recovering from the day's work. For a while, nothing was said. Nothing *needed* to be said, I thought. Everything was just right, and a conversation of smiles never felt better.

"So Shayla, how do you feel about how Meadowlark put you on-the-spot this morning?" Anne asked.

"I don't know Anne, part of me was totally embarrassed and terrified while the other part was honored and thrilled to be recognized." Before, I gave little thought to the incident because when it happened it was so overwhelming. But seated and relaxed with my new friends, I was able to ponder my feelings.

"Look Shayla, it doesn't make you strange if you have a crush on Meadowlark." All the girls laughed. "Everyone in the whole tree does, right?" She looked over at the two girls and several other bees that were sitting around, nodded their heads and giggling. Then I considered what she was saying and found my feelings toward Meadowlark to be just as she said—a crush. But because of the encounter I had with him privately in his nest the previous night, the crush was more enflamed and more like *true love*.

"Well, I guess I have some completion then," I said jokingly.

"You bet you do!" Elizabeth stood up. "I mean those thick wings and that golden chest—mmm." Elizabeth began to imitate his stature by puffing out her body, tipping her chin up and folding her arms at her sides like wings. She walked around pretending to be

57

like him, talking in a very low masculine voice as the other bees around pretended to go crazy over the imitated handsomeness.

"Oh he's so dreamy," said Anne who got up next to Elizabeth, "Oh Meadowlark sir, would you take me under your wing?"

"Why of course, my sister," Elizabeth said in a ridiculous deep voice. She wrapped her arm around Anne and began dancing around with her. I sat there looking at them in the midst of the laughter and merriment. To the best of my knowledge, they did not know of my actual encounter with Meadowlark that night under the moon. I thought it best never to mention it around them because I knew that I would never hear the end of it.

These girls and all the other bees, for the most part, knew exactly when to be strictly professional and when to have fun. And right now, it was all about fun.

"Come on Shayla, let's dance," said Emily pulling me up next to the dancing fools that were my new best friends. Emily and I held hands and danced around Elizabeth and Anne who were still caught up in the act. Emily spun me around, Anne was love-struck, Elizabeth was talking like Meadowlark and I was spinning out of control in absolute enjoyment.

I felt that we were embarrassing ourselves in front of the other bees but as it turned out, there were no objections and some bees actually joined us in our merry dancing. We danced and danced without a care in the world. During the dizziness, Elizabeth was clearly having the most fun impersonating Meadowlark and leading the dance. She made it clear to me that she was not only a good friend but also a social leader among all the bees.

Anne was like a twin to Elizabeth. She would always follow in Elizabeth's footsteps and back her all the way. Emily was more collected than the other girls. She always had plenty of fun just as they did, but also knew how to keep all of our feet on the ground. I loved each of them dearly and could not get enough.

"Oak be praised, let us dance until night," Elizabeth said to the dancing crowd, "Enjoy yourselves now sisters, there is much work ahead!"

THE SUN FLED THE SKY JUST AS THE DANCE CONCLUDED. We walked out of the Dining Hall completely dazed from our jovialities. Holding each other, the girls and I began walking down the Long Branch. Night was falling upon the Grand Oak once again as we witnessed the dark green leaves turn to a dense black. Everyone knew what time it was, so it was no surprise that every bee was headed in the same direction.

The Long Branch became filled with bees who strolled to the end of the branch where Meadowlark's nest was seated. The Long Branch became another large assembly of bees on which we all looked up to the nest where the twelve bees and Meadowlark were already waiting. The girls and I found seats in the back behind about ten rows of bees and sat down. The chatter among the bees was quite loud and disorientating, I thought as I looked around for Harriet who was nowhere to be found.

I wondered where she was during this night hour. She surely must be among us somewhere in this crowd, but I thought it curious that she was not amongst the governance in the nest. Perhaps she will turn up and I will find her, I supposed.

Inside the nest there was a circular conversation between the twelve bees and Meadowlark listening over their heads. I lifted my head up and around the bees in front of me to try and see what they were doing, but the noise was too great and the crowd was too large for me to see them. Then all of a sudden Meadowlark stood up in the nest and spread out both of his beautifully spotted wings and instantly silenced the crowd without a word.

The twelve bees stumbled up to the front edge of the nest where we all could see them. They held the long green scroll that was the precious map and unraveled it over the edge of the nest. By this wonderful display, the crowd began to scan the map and study its contents. The map comprised of several rectangular boxes with the largest of the boxes at the center, labeled in their strange leaf language that I was unable to read. Luckily one of the twelve began to explain the map to all of us.

"Now sisters, the map that we hold before you tonight displays the entire Oersted Farm from above." The bee used a short twig from the nest and pointed to a cloud-shaped drawing near the bottom of the leaf map. "Here is the Grand Oak situated as we all know the farthest from the Oersted Lair. In between us and the devil's chamber are the five box-hives shown here. Around the box-hives is the line of bushes where the imprisoned bees scavenge for most of their nectar."

I squinted to see the tiny box-hive drawings on the map and could just make out where the Meridian Hive was in relation to the Grand Oak. As it turned out, my former hive was conveniently the closest hive to the tree. I also never realized that the bushes that provided us with most of our nectar were so near to the box-hives.

"As for the Oersted Lair, we the Council have constructed another map specifically for this most crucial intelligence for our plans." A few of the bees stepped down into the nest and tried lifting the much larger leaf that required Meadowlark's assistance to lift. Soon, the twelve bees and Meadowlark were able to heave the leaf over the nest and put it on display for all the bees to see. The same bee that was explaining the previous map had to walk around to one side of the enormous leaf to continue the presentation.

"Our scouts were able to infiltrate the devil's lair through the chimney where Oersted occasionally puffs smoke and fire. Inside, the spies were able to survey the rooms and take note of the layout and structure of the lair. However, several minutes into the operation, Oersted discovered them and began swinging his bee-swatter, nearly blocking their escape. But the Council is proud to say that we sustained zero casualties during this mission."

The crowd applauded seriously and many clapped loudly for the honorable service of the spies. My only thoughts were of admiration for the courage of those brave bees. Perhaps one day I will show bravery of that magnitude, I thought.

"So if you'd look at the map here, we see that there are exactly seven rooms where the devil conducts his business. The spies have listened in on the conversations of Oersted and his children and have come to learn the names they use for these different zones. These names include the Kitchen, Bathroom, Dining Room, Living Room, and the three Bedrooms for himself and his two daughters." They pointed to the different drawn areas on the map as I struggled to understand what she meant by 'daughters' among other things—I simply was lost and confused.

"And adjacent to the house is the Shed where Oersted keeps all of his demonic beekeeping tools and poisons. There in the Shed is where he stores his smoke weapon and his blade for cutting and stealing the honeycombs from the box-hives." My eyes turned wide and my jaw dropped. Finally, I could perceive the landscape. My memories of flight throughout my life in the box-hives became clearer and less hazed.

"The Shed also houses the devices that Oersted uses to extract the honey from the honeycombs. He then places the honey in glass jars to be sent away to other devils in faraway lands." All of this sounded slightly farfetched at first but because this information was coming from the nest, it was hard not to believe. Then after holding the map out for a few seconds, the bees lifted the other map of the entire farm and placed it next to the larger leaf so that both could be seen by the audience.

"As you all know, we lack the beepower required to lead an assault on the Shed or the Lair. That is why tomorrow we begin our mission into each of the box-hives to free the prisoners and ultimately trigger this glorious revolution!" Everyone cheered and was encouraged by the Council as well as the look on Meadowlark's face that was his indescribable smile. "You all should expect word by morning from your Company Commanders concerning the objectives your regiments have been assigned to. Tomorrow will mark the beginning for the Meridian Hive's liberation—as we know, they need the immediate attention. And once the Meridian has been taken, we shall dispatch our liberation forces to the Luna Hive and so on."

Though the Council had decided on this plan in advance, they still had the courtesy to ask the mass of bees if there were any bees that objected to the plan. There was silence in response. The unanimity of all the bees was strong and so the decision of the Council was put in motion. As the twelve bees lined up next to the map in front of the nest, it became clear to me that they were in fact *also* the Company Commanders. One of the twelve stepped forward and pointed her twig at the Grand Oak on the map.

"By dawn, our combined liberation force will launch from the Grand Oak, flying low to the ground, avoiding attention, toward the Meridian Hive. At the entrance of the box-hive we will stand and present the prisoners with a gift of a Grand Oak honeycomb in exchange for their attention. They will be given the honey to help their sisters and will know that we are *not* savages. We will then enter their hive peacefully and educate their masses about the Grand Oak and the freedom that they can attain. And in the event this main force gets into trouble, we will have a backup regiment stationed in the tall grass just outside of the box-hive area to assist."

The reason for the additional regiment was clear in my mind. The Meridian Hive most likely has fallen to the martial control of the warriors simply because of the hysteria over the recent invasion. In other words, the panic that had ensued because of the wasp raid must have risen to a fevered pitch, making the Meridian Hive a hotspot for conflict if agitated.

Nevertheless, the Meridian prisoners were undoubtedly suffering from a lack of honey, thus the concept of the honeycomb gift was fairly appropriate. The overall plan seemed reasonable to me. The only problem was I did not know which Company I was assigned to because I was a new-bee. I looked over at the girls who were staring at the maps. In their company I felt safe, so I will most likely follow them on tomorrow's mission, I thought.

The meeting was quite basic but nonetheless exhilarating because we were to start our liberation campaign by morning. We all knew that after this meeting this land would never be the same again. All of our minds were filled with hope for a peaceful escape and transition for the prisoners down below. Even though I knew that many bees in the Meridian Hive hated me personally, I still felt a general compassion for the bees that I used to call my sisters in that box-hive. Perhaps tomorrow we might liberate them all and I might be forgiven by my sisters, I hoped.

It was then that I thought about Charlie and Rose. My heart sank as the discourse of the assembly was drowned out by my own thoughts. I felt great regret for not saving Rose and for losing Charlie's friendship because of my actions. The pity surged through my blood. I knew that I had to make things right. There was no possible way in my mind that I would miss the opportunity to join the bees on this mission. I had to redeem myself.

Then I realized that the Company Commanders had been talking, calling out names from a leaf list. Nearly none of the names I could relate so I did not pay much attention. Then out of the mess of names my head leaning up.

"—Marie-Claire, Kate, *Shayla*, Brook—" Suddenly my name was called and I did not know who my Company Commander was. I nudged my friend Elizabeth on the shoulder and whispered nervously to her.

"Hey *that's me*, but who is the bee calling those names?"

"That's Councilbee Andrea." I became nervous at the thought of not being accompanied by my friends during the mission and Elizabeth noticed this. "Don't worry Shayla, we'll meet up during the mission." I grasped Elizabeth's arm.

"But I don't know if I can do this," said I trembling.

"Shayla, you'll do fine, this is only the beginning anyway, there is no need to worry." Elizabeth reassured me enough so that I released my grip on her arm. I turned back toward the nest and sat uncomfortably. I then looked at Andrea who was to be my Company

Commander during the campaign, or at least for to-morrow's mission.

She was an older bee, but younger than Harriet by many moons. Her wings were long and straight with thick veins running down them. She looked worn out from the work of the Council but quite authoritative in her speech. She did not stutter or tarry when reading the names. Perhaps I was being too unwelcoming to change and too dependent on others—it was time to feel comfortable in my own skin, I thought as I looked at Andrea. Her mannerisms were calm and composed causing me to relax knowing that I was in good hands.

The names continued to be called until Andrea had finished her list. Then the next Councilbee began to read her list as we all waited and waited. Soon, all of the Company rosters were read and everyone knew who to go with and where to go. Being the new-bee, I only knew *who* I was to go with but not *where* to go. Looking around at the other bees and their movement around the crowd made me look like a helpless baby larva in the middle of a hectic day at work for the adult bees.

It was then that I realized my friends had left me to go line up with their Companies. I got up and struggled over to a group of bees that I thought were surrounding Andrea. As soon as I managed to shove myself over to the group through the thick crowd, I realized that I was in the wrong place and had to return to the chaos of bees and try to find Andrea. Every bee was lining up quicker than I could imagine and I did not want to be stuck in the open and embarrass myself not knowing where to line up.

Finally I found Andrea out of the clusters of bees and rushed over to the group. I got behind the first bee that I saw in the bunch and lined up behind her. All of the companies slowly became long lines behind the Councilbees in front of the nest where Meadowlark stood quietly. After a great last hustle, the bees were finally in twelve long columns standing still facing the nest. Meadowlark stepped out of the nest as the twelve lines split to create a path for him on the Long Branch.

"Companies, about face!" one of the Councilbees yelled causing the twelve rows to face inward toward the narrow path where Meadowlark was pacing. All was still except for the slow, clawing steps of Meadowlark's feet on the wood of the Long Branch. He walked silently without looking at any of us for a few moments. Then he stopped in the middle of the path and turned to one side.

"From here there is no turning back, my sisters. We have waited a long time for this moment to come, and now it is finally here. Our plans and preparations will be carried out by the flutter of your wings and the jabs of your stingers. Let this liberation process be swift and effective, for soon every bee from every hive will enjoy the taste of Oersted's blood. We have not come this far to fail, my sisters. By the mighty hand of the Grand Oak, we will succeed!"

Everyone's ears rattled from the sound of Meadowlark's stern voice. His spirit channeled discipline and excitement through our bodies as well as the desire to thrust the fist of vengeance into Oersted's cold demon heart.

"Rest well tonight, my sisters. The Grand Oak requires your strength tomorrow." And without another word, Meadowlark began walking down the Long Branch away from the nest as each of the Companies followed close behind him. I marched as well as I could with the other bees, lifting my legs at the right time and stepping in rhythm with my sisters.

We marched down the trunk toward the barracks at the base of the tree where the girls and I had trained. Down at the entrance to the barracks we stood on the moss valley between the thick roots and began our march down to the underground structure. Meadowlark stood above the relatively tiny entrance, staring at each of us as we entered its depths. Then as I walked inside, Meadowlark disappeared from sight.

Upon entering the tunnel again, I received the same feeling I experienced before with the girls after the assembly in the morning. I was scared of the terrible darkness that was intensified by the night. The thumping of the march down into the barracks echoed against the walls, giving me a great sense of awe at the might of our forces.

Inside the barracks, each of the twelve Companies separated into different rooms where there were individual cribs for all of us to sleep in. I entered one room with Andrea and the Company. We were told to find cribs to sleep in for the night. I quickly found a crib that was unoccupied and sat down on it. Within seconds the cribs next to mine were filled as the Company hastily poured into the room.

The dim lights that emanated from the few honey lamps in the room were closed up and we were told by Andrea to go right to sleep. I settled into my crib and looked around at the other bees lying beside me. Many of them were able to follow the orders and drift straight to sleep, however, I was not among them. The anxiety of tomorrow's mission kept me awake for a little while before I joined them all in the great slumber before the glorious morning.

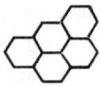

"WAKE UP YOU BEES, TIME TO GET BUSY!" SOMEONE shouted into our quarters. I tensed my eyes at the light that was poured into the room. When I looked to see what was happening, I could see a line of honey being dispensed out into the middle of the room. If that doesn't wake a bee up in the morning I don't know what does.

All of the bees including myself jumped out of our cribs and began feasting on the honey rations dropped at the center of the barracks. We stuffed our faces with the rich golden honey and conjured up great morning energy. As we were eating together rapidly, Andrea stepped into the room and called out to us.

"We march at the call of Meadowlark, bees, eat your fill before we move!" This news caused all of the bees to rush out of bed and eat madly before the march. Disoriented, I ate wildly and began to fear over-eating that might slow me down during the mission. I reluctantly pulled myself away from the pile of honey as other bees filled in my space. I stood up looking at the feasting bees holding my stomach that I was afraid would burst. They all ate to their hearts' delight that morning.

71

Luckily, I was alright and relaxed knowing that I would not be slowed down by the rations. I moved toward the door of the barracks and stood near Andrea. The Councilbee stood there watching the bees, listening closely for the Meadowlark's chirp that would initiate the mission any moment now. I quickly licked my hair and antennas into a presentable fashion and joined the line that was preparing to exit the barracks at the drop of a leaf.

We stood there like warriors anticipating the call to action from our beloved leader. Our combined sense of time was thrown and nearly every bee finished their morning meal, quickly joining the line behind their sisters. I looked around at the faces of the bees that I was to march with. None of them looked like soldiers or killers. We all were simply regular honeybees with strong passions and motivated spirits.

Then suddenly the sound of Meadowlark's loud call shocked the earth resonating through the barracks' tunnels. We all heard it and locked into a marching formation. At the command of Commander Andrea, we began our quickstep out of the barracks and into the light of the morning. The rumble of footsteps launched our Company and all the others out onto the shady moss where the morning dew drenched the soil.

All the twelve companies gathered at the base of the Grand Oak and organized. It was then that three of the Companies split off from our group and began taking up positions in the tall grass close to the tree. The remaining nine Companies formed up into one large phalanx square and patiently awaited orders. Then all of a sudden a giant piece of honeycomb came from the top of the Grand Oak. It was Meadowlark bringing us the gift for the Meridian Hive.

Afraid of being crushed by the massive honeycomb, we all stood in the phalanx nervously. But Meadowlark began flapping his powerful wings, slowing himself to a hover over us. Many of the bees at the center of the formation were told to take the honeycomb and hold it above our heads. Luckily I did not have to be encumbered with the burden because I was in the Company nearest to the right flank of the phalanx.

The middle Companies held the generous gift up high and the Commanders said that we were ready to march. Then Andrea took the lead and ordered us forward. We marched slowly through the grass and over roots until we touched the dirt ground that marked the box-hive prison zone. As we gained momentum, our phalanx hopped into flight and quickly reached the bush line that surrounded the box-hives. It was time to go over the top.

Following behind the flight paths of our Commanders, we propelled ourselves over the tall bushes and came back down on the other side. The entire battalion patiently waited for the moment when all of the bees were carried safely over the bush line with the honeycomb intact. Finally, everyone was on the other side and we were able to continue our low flight toward the Meridian Hive.

I looked forward over the bees in front of me and saw the Meridian Hive standing high over our heads, reflecting bright light down onto us from its bleak white walls. The battalion neared closer and closer to the box-hive with intense caution and awareness. To the best of our abilities we tried not to create a disturbance that would stir the box-hive's bees into violent action against us.

We approached the Meridian Hive and halted our march at a safe distance from the Public Porch. I looked up at the top of the hive from the ground and saw several bees swarming around patrolling the airspace. Then some of them noticed our large numbers and swiftly returned into the box. For a while there was no activity. We looked straight ahead of us and saw that the entrance at the foot of the hive where bodies had been stacked was in complete darkness from the shadows. Very few, if any, *live* bees lingered on the Public Porch at the base of the Meridian.

Then as we stood there motionless, a wall of warriors authoritatively appeared on the Public Porch. They seemed to be extremely hostile and apprehensive. Stingers drawn, they were prepared to defend the box-hive at all cost. The looks that they gave us were grim with the same hate that they would radiate to any wasp if seen around here. They saw that we were unarmed and holding the large honeycomb above our heads.

Among the ranks we stood still, allowing the nine Commanders to step forward slowly toward the Meridian warriors. In a line in front of us, our leaders sauntered up close to the warriors and stood at wing's length. The warriors stood on the incline of the Public Porch towering over the tiny Councilbees below their heads. Without warning, another group of warriors and militia bees emerged from the entrance of the box-hive and reinforced the line of warriors. All was quiet on the Public Porch until Andrea broke the silence.

"Noble warriors of the Meridian Hive, we the bees of the Grand Oak come to you in peace." The warriors just stood there scanning all of our faces, especially the faces of our leaders. They examined nearly every inch of us before one of them began to speak.

"What brings you here, savage?" One of the largest warriors who I had vaguely known before my departure from the Meridian Hive seemed to stand taller than any of the other warriors in the line. The warrior looked at Andrea closely eye-to-eye, scraping her antennae across the Councilbee's face. I looked on in terror as Andrea remained calm and unmoved by the warrior's intimidation.

"The Council of the Grand Oak has decided to bestow upon the Meridian Hive this gift of honey that will show our sorrow for your hive's heavy losses and precarious condition." My eyes wandered off to the piled up bodies on the Public Porch that reeked of decay. The warrior then came close to Andrea and spoke to her very severely.

"Don't you dare tell us about our situation, *you cannibal*! The Meridian Hive is secure no thanks to you savage barbarians." The warrior turned back toward the mob of bees behind her and motioned for them to move forward. The bees quickly rushed past the line of Councilbees and lifted the honeycomb off of the shoulders of the middle bees carrying it. They tugged the honeycomb up the Public Porch and into the hive where it disappeared inside the shady darkness.

"Now that you have taken our gift, we would like permission into your hive to speak with the populace. You see we seek to free you bees from—" The warrior laughed.

"From what, you savage? The only thing our bees seek to be free from are your petty lies and deceptions about that damned tree you worship! Our bees are in good hands now because of us warriors who have filled in the gap where our common honeybees have lacked. The bees of the Meridian Hive have nothing to fear now that we are in power. Queen Meridian herself wishes this so. We do not require any 'freedom' from you barbarians nor do we welcome you into our hive. Now take this monstrosity of ruffians behind you back to your beloved tree and leave us the hell alone!"

The warrior backed up with her supportive mob of disillusioned bees back into the hive, closing the entranceway behind them. I looked up to the portholes of the hive where many of the box-hive's bees were watching hopelessly from the window with their arms out begging for our help without buzzing a word. All of us were shocked. Our leaders stood still. All of the Councilbees refrained from immediate response to what had just occurred. I looked to my fellow bees and saw disappointed looks on many of their faces. Our plan was failing and we all knew something had to be done.

The Company Commanders quickly turned back around to us and ordered a casual retreat back to the bush line to regroup. The entire battalion flew irritated back to the shady bush line where we gathered in a semicircle around the nine officers. They looked at all of us as we sat down to receive their orders. Once it was quiet, Andrea stepped forward to address the battalion.

"I need two volunteers!" Instantly several bees rushed to the forefront of the group and two of them were chosen by the officers. "Deliver this message to both the reserve Companies and Meadowlark: 'The warrior coup appears to have taken over the operations of the box-hive. These warriors may be the greatest threat to the Meridian prisoners at this time. We seek permission to enter the prison by force to free the prisoners.' *You* ask this permission of Meadowlark, and *you* inform the reserve Companies that we may require backup if Meadowlark answers affirmative—go!"

The two messenger bees shot off into the air, flying in separate directions. The rest of the Companies sat waiting for instruction. Just as the messengers flew out of sight, Andrea and the other Commanders stepped close to the semicircle of bees.

"Alright, now if Meadowlark approves of this, we must be prepared to take the proper precautions before entering the box by force. We have to make it clear to the Meridian bees that we are here to liberate them and *not* to invade. In the event that, upon entrance, the warriors attack us in defense, we must be prepared to hold them back while the majority of our force pushes into all combs of the hive to free the bees inside." Andrea then looked back at the other officers who nodded at her statements. Then she turned back to the Companies.

"It is not with great pleasure that we have to oppose the warriors of the Meridian. It was our goal to free *all* of the bees in the box-hives and not just the citizenry. But it appears that the warrior society, at least inside the Meridian Hive, has become a danger to the regular honeybees of the box. Our main priority now is to release the bees that are trapped inside before we will be able to liberate the warriors as well."

Then, just moments after the messengers had left, Meadowlark dropped out of the sky and landed behind the Commanders. His dramatic entrance caught everyone's eye.

"I have received your message, my sisters, and have returned with an answer." The messenger bee that had delivered the message to him returned exhausted moments after Meadowlark's swift arrival. "No bee shall lift up their stinger against a fellow bee! I shall hold the warriors off while you brave bees liberate your imprisoned sisters. We haven't much time, let us move now before our morning morale vanishes." All of the officers looked at each other and ordered us to stand up and march back to the Public Porch the same as we came the first time.

Meadowlark hopped back into the air and flew high enough above our heads to blur the brown spots on his handsome feathers. We lined up again and began marching toward the Meridian Hive. Our step became more angry and confident as we re-approached the Public Porch. As we came close again I looked up at the portholes where crowds of trapped bees hailed our return. The warriors inside must have noticed this disturbance and pushed them aside from the windows. They saw us and rushed back down to the entrance to meet us again face-to-face.

Our lines held strong in front of the Public Porch in the same position that we had arrived in, except this time we would not be disrespected. That same hot-headed warrior bee stomped out of the box-hive with his stinger clearly visible and his warrior posse right behind him.

"Well look who it is. The savages have returned to taste their own blood." All of us stood still—*peacefully* as Meadowlark instructed while I trembled in fear that we would end up clashing with the warriors stinger-to-stinger. "Any last words before we add your carcasses to the walls of our hive?"

Then suddenly two massive claws plunged out of the sky, clasped the warrior and threw him back toward the mob behind him knocking down several other warriors. Meadowlark had shocked the warriors at the mere sight of his strength.

"It's monster! It's a bee-eater!" cried one of the frightened warriors. Meadowlark stood firmly on the wood of the porch and began flapping his powerful wings quickly at the mob causing many to roll away in the strong wind. He continued this maneuver and turned his head to see us all.

"Go, now!" he yelled to us over the great air current that nearly deafened all the bees. The Commanders lifted their wings and led us in our charge into the box-hive. The warrior bees were so shocked by the might of Meadowlark that they were unable to stop us from entering the hive. We rushed in as one large mass of screaming bees bent on delivering our sisters from bondage to freedom. The darkness inside the hive amongst all the chaos was the first sign that something was wrong. Usually this hive, where I have spent most of my life, shined with golden honeycombs all over, but now it was nearly empty.

Inside there were dead bodies scattered all around, wax crumbling from above, and starving bees on the ground gripping their stomachs. As we appeared to them in the chaos of our entry, they crawled toward us miserably for rescue. The Companies were quickly divided up and sent to each layer of the hive to gather the bees. Andrea pushed our Company to liberate the bees at the base of the hive where they needed the most help.

The bees that I had been following the whole time jumped around the box-hive grabbing the suffering bees and pulling them out of the hive. I leaped to one bee that was crawling toward me for assistance. I grasped her with my legs and pulled both our weight into the air below the low ceiling, and then launched out of the hive.

The light hit my eyes again. I saw that the three reserve companies had arrived and had formed a defensive circle with an empty space in the middle. Bees were carrying bees into the middle of this circle to be dropped off and protected by the reservists. I pulled my fellow bee over to the circle and placed her slowly down to the dirt as I heard her sandy starving breath inhale and exhale fearfully. After I put her down, a bee from the circle picked her back up and swiftly carried her high into the air to the Grand Oak where the freed prisoners were being taken.

I looked back at the Public Porch where Meadowlark was throwing and swatting warriors off of his feathers. As the warriors tried to latch onto Meadowlark's body they were quickly thrown off by his powerful wing muscles. And every time some of the warriors tried to stop the liberating bees from exiting the hive with the prisoners, Meadowlark would wave his wings and clear a path for the bees to escape.

I headed back into the dim, frantic hive and continued to pull bees out to the drop-off zone. We made great progress and remained fairly organized on the outside knowing that we had Meadowlark's protection. Back inside the box we had to continuously push the dead bodies out of our way to extract the live bees. It was only on my third trip into the box-hive that I realize how horrid the stench from the decaying bodies was. I had to push those thoughts out of my mind as we helped the deprived bees out into the light.

Luckily, not all of the bees of the Meridian were in as bad a condition as those at the bottom lying with the dead. I saw a few groups of bees rush out of the hive and takeoff without any help from our liberation force. But most required some sort of attention from our bees. The starving, the weak, the wounded, the dying— they all needed our help. Soon, nearly every bee was carried out of the nest and our companies began to evacuate from the box. We picked up every bee we could from the middle of the circle and in one combined retreat, we pulled back to the Grand Oak.

As we tugged the entire populace of the Meridian Hive up to the Grand Oak, all the branches became makeshift shelters and infirmaries for the suffering bees. I landed with my Company carrying a wounded bee and brought her to a drop-off area where bees were being medically assisted. There were leaves laid out for the wounded to lie on while bees from the tree rushed to help the wounded and dying first. I placed my bee down and looked up. I was surprised to see Harriet standing there helping a wounded bee that was suffering from a wound to the abdomen.

I watched for a moment as Harriet held the bee down and began to mend the bee's wound with wax just as she did when I was wounded. The bee was bleeding profusely as Harriet rushed to seal up the long gash. It looked like she had been slashed and cut open by the stinger of another honeybee. I wondered where she would have acquired this wound because I was fairly certain that none of the Grand Oak bees violently assaulted any Meridian bee during the exodus.

Looking around I saw that most of the bees from the box-hive and the liberation force had successfully landed in the Grand Oak. The tree was filled with bees that scrabbled from branch to branch while many suffered. The largest problem our liberation force had to deal with was feeding the starving bees. When I looked down the Long Branch I could see that the Dining Hall had become a massive disarray of ravenous bees. It appeared that nearly every prisoner had been starved in the Meridian Hive as they barged into the honeycombs and ate like beasts.

"Shayla!" Harriet noticed me standing about. I turned around and she looked up at me. "Get over here, I need your help!" I quickly rushed over to Harriet who was holding her patient down with all of her arms and legs. "Shayla, the ball of wax behind you, pass it to me!" I turned back and saw a wad of wax on the wood. I swiped it up and passed it to Harriet. She took it from me and pulled me down to kneeling with her next to the struggling bee. "Now, hold her down, I have to sow this wax, don't let that cut open up again!"

I frantically grabbed the bee and held her down as she struggled and screamed from the pain of the wound. Harriet let go of the patient and I had to use all of my strength to keep her down. Harriet ran the wax through her teeth and created a line of thread that she then brought over to the patient. She continued to sew the wound shut with both of her hands while I held the bee on the ground. Because of our teamwork, the wound was closed and we stopped the bleeding.

"You're going to be alright, hold still, my sister," Harriet tenderly said to the bee. She then asked me to grab a piece of leaf behind her and wrap it around the bee's wound area. We wrapped her up and placed her in a crib inside one of the nearby hives. The bee began to lie still in the crib, in pain but comfortable enough to control her movements.

We emerged from the hive and both looked around at all of the bees swarming around, helping other bees. Soon it became apparent that nearly every single bee from the Grand Oak was helping their fellow sister in some way. We looked for other places where we were needed and had difficulty locating bees that weren't already being attended to. It appeared that the liberation effort of the Meridian Hive was successful for the most part and the integration of the freed bees into the lifestyle and freedom of the Grand Oak will have to begin soon. But there was one thing that was missing—Meadowlark!

"Harriet, where is Meadowlark?!" We looked around the tree and saw no sign of him as it appeared that he did not return to the tree as we did. We looked down from the Long Branch and saw in the distance his wings flapping and struggling against the malicious warriors. I looked at Harriet with terror in my face. "We have to help him!" I shouted.

"No, Shayla! Meadowlark can handle himself against those bastards, and besides, the last thing we need to do is fight against other honeybees!" I looked back down at Meadowlark fighting the warriors and saw him jumping about in fierce combat.

"But he is in trouble, those warriors are *killers*!" My blabbering made little sense to Harriet who knew Meadowlark's plan much better than I did at the time.

"Shayla, the Grand Oak will protect Meadowlark, have no fear, I am sure he will be alright." She placed her hand on my shoulder partly to comfort me and partly to clamp my wings down to prevent me from flying over to assist him in combat.

84

I did however continue to watch as Meadowlark fought gallantly with the crazed warriors down below. Though he was much more powerful than any one warrior, the warriors in conjunction began attacking him from all sides at the same time which nearly over-whelmed him. But Meadowlark leaped into flight again and began flying around the Meridian Hive in circles to stir the warriors into pursuing him. They followed close behind him in a swarm that flew together in formation to try and bring down the mischievous bird to the ground.

Then Meadowlark drew the warriors toward the Grand Oak, attempting to force them into surrender. In a matter of seconds, Meadowlark reached the lower part of the tree and I repositioned myself on the edge of the Long Branch to look down below to watch him. His stylish maneuvers greatly rattled the warriors. Cir-cling the circumference of the Grand Oak, Meadowlark created confusion among the warriors and threw many into disorientation from his radical flight paths.

Soon all of the bees on the Long Branch, who were well enough to fight, including many of the freed pris-oners that returned from the Dining Hall with full stomachs, looked on at Meadowlark's spectacular aerial performance. Then suddenly when everyone was watching, Meadowlark tipped his flight path skyward and pulled the pursuing warriors up to the branches of the tree where hundreds of bees were lying in wait. Meadowlark quickly came up to the Long Branch and landed on the wood behind literally hundreds of stand-ing bees. Then the warriors came up and were shocked to see the mass of bees gathered on the Long Branch and all of the surrounding subsequent branches above and below. The warriors were trapped.

Meadowlark saw that the warriors were in one tight swarm and jumped up to catch them. He grabbed all of the warriors with his full wingspan and firmly held them within his grasp. All of the bees cheered for Meadowlark and jeered at the warriors. The trapped warriors struggled and flapped their wings hopelessly inside of Meadowlark's feathers; we all knew that there was no escape for them now.

Instead of crushing and killing the warriors as he easily could have, Meadowlark brought them over to his nest as we all looked on without any comprehension of his plan. Harriet and I both decided to go over to the nest with a group of bees to watch what Meadowlark was going to do to the warriors and assist him if need be, after all, there were hostile killer warriors right in the hive among us. Meadowlark stepped into the gully of the nest as a large group of the bees surrounded the edge of the nest looking down upon the warriors.

He opened his wings and released them onto the floor. They all looked terrified and pathetic to all of us. Some of the bees laughed and taunted them while others stood ready to put them down if they tried to fight. Meadowlark stood high above them and dipped his head at each of them, skimming his sharp beak passed their faces. Meadowlark had taken several stings to the chest and back but none of the lacerations seemed to hurt him.

"Why are you so frightened? If I was going to kill you, don't you think I would have done so already? Do not be scared, I am going to make this easy for you and give you some options to pick from. Your first choice is to lay down your arms and join us for the cause of freedom in the Grand Oak—which I would humbly suggest myself. And the other choice would be to fly as fast as you can away from this place before I tear you limb-from-limb for what you have done to your own bees." Meadowlark saw that many bees had gathered around the nest who had been oppressed by the tyrannical warriors and came to see the warriors face justice at last.

The warriors looked around at the bees and Meadowlark hopelessly, knowing that there was no escape for them. They realized that they would have to comply with whatever Meadowlark offered them. Then they all looked at each other and unanimously agreed.

"We're sorry, we're sorry, please forgive us, spare us, *spare* us!" Meadowlark smiled, then picked them all up again in one of his wings as they all gasped in fear.

Meadowlark flew with the warriors down to a dead branch on the Grand Oak and placed them in a crevasse between a split-branch. He placed them inside the small prison-like space and told them that they would be given no food for one whole day; like the ex-hostage bees from the box, they too would feel the pains of being famished. It was time for them to suffer duly before they would be able to join the Grand Oak with their *true* spirits.

Most of the bees, especially the freed bees, wanted to see the warriors killed, or better yet, *eaten* by Meadowlark, but we all came to understand that this punishment was for the best. We might require their service in our campaign along the way, but only if their hearts and minds were without corruption and pure.

The crowd around the nest dispersed and everyone went back to their business helping other bees recuperate. Some bees like the ones that crowded around the nest seemed to be already adjusting to the Grand Oak's lifestyle and the profound energy that was accessible to all. Sometimes I could hardly tell the difference between any bees in the tree. The Meridian Hive was finally one with the Grand Oak.

HARRIET AND I WENT BACK TO CHECK ON THE BEE THAT we had cared for moments before in her crib. As we reentered the small hive, we saw that the patient was sitting upright, holding her wound. She immediately saw us and looked at Harriet.

"Thank you for saving me," said the bee in a most sensitive timbre to Harriet.

"You are quite welcome, my sister. You are safe here in the Grand Oak. Please remain in this hive for this day and night before you begin to crawl again." Harriet came next to the bee and sat down. Then I stepped forward to Harriet.

"Is there anything else you need, Harriet," I asked.

"Yes, Shayla, grab that honey over there and come sit with us." I picked up the honey and sat beside Harriet in front of the wounded bee that was eying the honey as I used to eye nectar-filled flowers.

"Here," Harriet dipped her hand into the honey and took out small portions to give to the hungry patient. "Eat this, but eat it slowly." The bee began to eat the small droplets of honey and began to sit more comfortably knowing that she would not starve in the

89

Grand Oak. After the bee was sufficiently relaxed, Harriet began to ask her questions.

"What is your name?"

"My name is Rae," she said, "I am a flapper; I keep the hive cool when it gets hot."

"It's nice to meet you Rae, my name is Harriet and this here is Shayla who you might know."

"Shayla?"

"That's right." Rae turned to me.

"Are you that bee that some have called a traitor and deserter?"

"Yes…" A frown came upon my face. Rae looked at me and shook her head.

"After I saw you and your comrades save our lives down there, I know the rumors to be *untrue*." I smiled and blushed. "The way that you have liberated and carried us to this place shows that you are *no* traitor. You came back for us, you and these bees that we called savages." Rae smiled, shook her head again, and turned to Harriet. "Even though I don't quite understand where I am right now, I know for sure that you bees are *not* savage cannibals as most of us thought."

"What happened down there, with the warriors, how did they come to power as they did?" I asked. The smile disappeared from Rae's face.

"Well, after most of our honey was stolen by the wasps during the raid, everyone became desperate and needy for food. Once we consumed nearly all of our remaining honey, there were brawls all across the Meridian over the last resources. *That's* when the warriors took over. Seeing as they were the most powerful and well-armed bees in the hive, they seamlessly began hoarding the remaining honey for themselves at the expense of the common bee."

"That's terrible, what did the warriors do to you?" I asked.

"The warriors kept us locked up in the hive. They only rationed honey to the most important bees and workers while others began to starve. Before you all saved us, we were cowering inside, afraid of the sharp stingers of the warriors who policed us into submission. And when you came with that huge piece of honeycomb, the warriors took it up to their corner and hogged it all for themselves. When you came back the second time, I remember seeing them wiping the honey off of their lips to seem as if they were the honorable ones."

"Bastards..." Harriet whispered.

"Say, did Queen Meridian make it out?" asked Rae. She saw that we both did not have the answer. "Well I pray that she did, because gossip has been going around saying that the warriors managed to kill her during their takeover." Rae paused for a moment and then resumed. "I don't want to believe that..." Harriet took in hand some more of the honey and fed it to Rae.

"Worry about yourself right now, Rae, you are in good hands here." Rae ate the honey, slowly savoring it and began to think deeply. Then she began to look around and started to panic.

"I don't know where I am, I have to go back to my comb, I have to work—I *have to* work!" Harriet put her arms around Rae.

"Rae, calm down, you have to sit still or else your wound will open up again! Everything will be explained, you just need to relax now and trust us. We saved you from that hellish place and now you do not have to worry about working as hard as you did. The Grand Oak does not need flappers to keep it cool— you can relax. When you are ready, you can perform some other job that suits you here, but now you must rest." Harriet held her down until she finally stopped jerking around. Harriet stood up, grabbed my hand to exit the hive and we both left Rae to rest and recover.

Outside, the commotion was still persisting. Those that needed prolonged care were receiving it while some bees already thought to give a tour of the Grand Oak to the new-bees. Harriet looked down the Long Branch and then turned back to me.

"If you would excuse me," said Harriet as she hopped into flight and flew down the Long Branch to wherever she was looking. Her business was more important than mine, I knew for sure.

Feeling somewhat lonely, I looked around for Elizabeth and the other girls that were such great friends to me. With the now greatly increased population of the Grand Oak, it was hard to find anyone in the throng of bees. I peeked for a moment back into the small hive where Rae was lying still. She looked depressed but thankful for Harriet and the Grand Oak that she was alive and had a place to stay. Looking at her, I wondered if the rumor about the warriors killing the Queen was accurate. What a horrible turn of events, I thought, assuming that the rumor was true.

I took a stroll down the Long Branch passing many bustling bees along the way. Small hives were becoming overpopulated by the new-bees, so new ones were already being built by the combined efforts of the passionate bees who now worked as one. On a side-branch that forked off of the Long Branch, there were several bees standing, looking down at the box-hives below. I walked over to them and stood on the thin branch behind them. One of the few bees turned around and spotted me standing there confused.

"Hey Shayla, c'mon over here." I realized it was Elizabeth and the other girls that turned around to see me. I was surprised to see them there amidst all of the commotion.

"Hey girls, what's up?" I approached them and sat down. They were all attentively watching the box-hives and the operations of the farm. I looked out and saw the sun beating down on the five hives as well as the large structures that I started to understand were Oersted's Lair and his Shed.

All of the hives, except for the Meridian, were active and appeared to be gathering and producing honey as usual. The Meridian Hive, though completely destroyed and motionless, did not draw the attention of any bee from the other box-hives on the farm.

"What are you guys doing over here?" I asked Elizabeth.

"Most of the bees in our Company were told to monitor the status of the box-hives and watch out for Oersted." The devil's image appeared in my mind.

"It is almost time for the devil to check the boxes," said Emily looking at the Lair while holding a piece of leaf above her eyes.

"Maybe if you try hard enough, Shayla, you will be able to see Oersted's true form," suggested Anne sliding closer to me on the branch.

"I don't know if I can, but I'll try." We all patiently waited for the sun to reach the right degree in the sky that would signal the emergence of the devil from his lair. We waited and waited for a very long time, just watching every tiny movement of the farm from the flow of the grass to the shadows cast by the sun.

Then out of the Oersted Lair appeared a gargantuan figure standing under the high overhang of the structure's roof. The monster closed the door to the lair and stepped into the light. The colossal creature stomped around, creating tremors with every step. It menacingly walked across the grass to the Shed where all of the evil tools are said to be kept. The monster entered the Shed and disappeared from sight.

Finally I had seen Oersted himself for the first time. When he disappeared into the Shed, I looked over at the other bees walking along the Long Branch. I realized that only the hardened free-bees were able to perceive Oersted while the new-bees passed by oblivious to his existence. Just as I had seen him, they all will know of his presence soon enough.

I turned back over and looked at the Shed. Oersted came out of the structure with two objects, one in each hand. In his left hand there was a cylindrical metallic object that glistened in the light. In the devil's right hand he held another shimmering object that was a long sharp blade. From the container held in his left hand, puffs of smoke arose to dance as they ascended to the sky.

The creature began to move toward the box-hives with patience and steadiness. It opened the gate through the bush line and entered the vicinity of the box-hives. Inside the perimeter, the devil went to survey each box-hive and inspect its contents. Oersted placed his tools on the dirt floor and lifted a heavy block off the top of a hive with bees swarming all around. He removed the lid of the box-hive and placed it on the ground.

The devil then took up his metal cylinder and began spraying smoke all over the top of the hive where the bees were swarming. All of the bees stopped swarming so madly and returned to the box. Their obedience to Oersted was strict and absolute once they were sprayed.

"What is he spraying on them?" I asked Elizabeth.

"We don't know what exactly the smoke is made of, but we sure as hell know it *can't* be good," said Elizabeth staying focused on Oersted. "Those poor bees don't have a clue what is being done to them."

Oersted used his knife to pry out individual sheets of the box-hive. The sheets were covered with bees attending to their daily business. Oersted sprayed the smoke again and again to disperse the bees from the sheet. What was left was a nearly completed honeycomb that radiated a bright yellow shine over the box.

Oersted inspected the sheet and placed it back in the box.

He placed the wooden cover back on the hive and replaced the stone block on top. Oersted continued this process for all of the box-hives, spraying each one, and examining the production and status of each hive without sympathy for the bees in bondage. It appeared that the devil actually enjoyed spraying the smoke over the bees to disorient them in the haze.

Then Oersted happily walked over to the Meridian Hive. There he removed the stone block and uncovered the lid. What he saw made him drop his tools on the ground. The box-hive was totally empty; no honey, no combs, no bees. Oersted became mad and overwrought as he flipped through the empty layers of the box-hive. He must have been wondering: where have all of his Meridian slave-bees gone?

Oersted's rage drew him to search all around the five hives and yet he found nothing. Those slaves that worked to produce one-fifth of 'his' honey were now free-bees in the Grand Oak and there was nothing he could do about it. The girls and the other bees next to me watched Oersted attentively and took note of his reaction. We all could see that Oersted was infuriated by this great mystery.

"It looks like we've sent a strong message to the devil," said Elizabeth in a serious tone. Oersted stormed back into his lair, stomping the ground feverishly. Elizabeth turned around at the Long Branch and then looked at me with a strange smile. "Let the games begin."

Some of the bees on the side-branch got up and left, but the girls and I continued to watch the land. After a few more moments, Oersted returned again from the lair with a bowl of some sort holding a yellow material inside. It was a mush of a dull yellow, not golden enough to be honey.

"What is that?" I asked Elizabeth.

"Fake honey—intelligence says that Oersted calls it *'apple sauce'*." Oersted came back to the Meridian Hive and placed the dish on top of the stone block. "Damn it, it's a lure—we need to have that assembly *now*! Anne, Emily, May—inform the Company Commanders."

"Roger that!" They all buzzed out and went to find the Company Commanders. It became clear that Oersted had just placed a desirable bait to re-enslave the Meridian bees. We realized that we had to educate the new-bees before they would notice the apple sauce and fly back to their prison. Elizabeth stood up and turned to me.

"*You and I*, Shayla, are going to Meadowlark."

"Us?!"

"Yes *us*, let's go." We jumped into flight and headed toward the split-branch where Meadowlark was punishing and disciplining the warriors. We landed right behind him as he was jamming his beak into the wood around them, instilling fear with every thrust.

"Meadowlark sir, a word with you please, sir?" Elizabeth's words made Meadowlark rather cross because she and I were interrupting his delicate business. He swung a final thrust into the split-branch and the warriors shook with fear. He then turned around and saw both of us. Instantly he became calm and composed himself as he always did.

"My dears, how can I assist you?"

"Sir, it appears that Oersted has just placed a trap on top of the Meridian Hive. A dish of apple sauce—" Meadowlark cut Elizabeth off. Without hesitation, Meadowlark knew exactly what he needed to do.

"Get to your Companies and rally at the nest!"

"Yes sir!" we both responded as we all leaped into the air. The warriors remained there in the crack of the split-branch shivering from fear. It was evident that they did not require any surveillance to keep them in-check.

We returned to the Long Branch and Meadowlark swooped all around the tree, chirping to the bees to assemble in front of the nest immediately. All of the free-bees knew exactly where to go and most helped the new-bees assemble with them. Elizabeth and I went our separate ways to our Companies and lined up quickly in front of the nest. I quickly sat down and looked around me. The free-bees were sitting in straight lines behind their Company Commanders while the new-bees sat among the lines and around in clusters.

Meadowlark landed in the center of the nest after most of the bees had arrived. Several others including a few Company Commanders came belated to the edge of the nest where they then stood attentively. Though Meadowlark may have appeared as a bee-eater at first to the new-bees during the liberation, he now was well-loved by all because of his actions. Andrea and all the

Councilbees stood still, waiting for Meadowlark to speak.

"Greetings my friends and thank you for being at attention for this urgent announcement. With the Meridian prison completely abandoned, our great enemy, Oersted, is prepared to take action to draw you new-bees back to your old prison ways. I have received word that the devil has placed a lure to bring back those of you new-bees. This lure is a fraudulent appetizer of sweet apple sauce that would force you new-bees to reenter the prison that was your box-hive."

I looked around and could see that much of this talk was being understood by the free-bees but to the new-bees, none of it made sense. Meadowlark glanced at all of the new-bees seated mainly at the back of the crowd.

"Though now that our numbers are greater, we must hold together and cutback on our honey usage for the time being before the new hives can be built to sustain us all comfortably. I implore all of you new-bees to hold strong with the Grand Oak. Your box-hive that you once called home is now unsustainable and a deceitful trap of your master Oersted who wants to see you enslaved again. We in the Grand Oak want to see you free among us and desire freedom for the rest of the box-hives that can only be liberated with our combined efforts."

The new-bees looked around at each other and some who had not made acquaintances with other free-bees began to gaze out over the Long Branch to see the dish of apple sauce. Those that did look pondered leaving the Grand Oak. Then Andrea stood in front of the other Councilbees and spoke.

"Every bee in the Grand Oak at this time must share their keep of honey only until the new hives can be constructed for our growing population." Then Meadowlark added to her statement.

"There is enough space in the Grand Oak for every bee. Soon you will all have homes of your own. We oblige you to join our society and help free the rest of your sisters from the other box-hive prisons." Meadowlark could see that not many of the new-bees understood what his terms were or even what he meant by 'box-hives' but Meadowlark already had plans for them. "Throughout the day, we will begin to hold educational meetings at the High Branch for all new-bees in the Grand Oak. We all must know the truth, and the truth will set this entire farm free. Oak be praised!"

"Oak be praised!" nearly all of the free-bees shouted back. Meadowlark and the Council began to make their way toward the High Branch of the Grand Oak where educational meetings would be held immediately. Once they had left, the crowd started to disperse. As I walked away from the crowd with my Company, I saw a group of new-bees staring at the apple sauce down on the Meridian Hive. I looked at them nervously.

They gave each other one last glance and took off toward the box-hives. Andrea and another Company Commander that was leading us across the Long Branch saw this and shouted at them.

"No! Stay and hold together! It's a trap! *It's a trap!*" they shouted to all of the new-bees. Looking down the

Long Branch you could see several new-bees retreating back to their old prison to taste the apple sauce dish that was set out for them. Our Companies were ordered to try and hold the new-bees back and we stopped many from leaving, but a few managed to get away. It was not our intention to keep them against their will but rather to save them from falling for the deception below.

By the time we relaxed the crowd, the fleeing bees had already reached the apple sauce. We all turned to them and saw them from afar devouring the sweet honey substitute. For many new-bees it looked appealing and delicious, but to any experienced free-bee, it looked like a horrible trap that would soon consume *them* just as they consumed *it*.

Soon all of the free-bees that were contemplating leaving began to gasp and forget all of their ideas of desertion. The bees that were eating the apple sauce began to sink into it and suffocate until death. The trap had made short work of the bees who only knew slavery and could not handle freedom. Those that stayed and did not flee knew that the Grand Oak was the only safe place to be as they all headed for the High Branch to hear Meadowlark and the Council's words of wisdom.

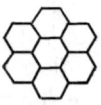

THE HIGH BRANCH WAS ABSOLUTELY FILLED TO THE BRIM. Bees were practically standing on top of each other to see Meadowlark and the Councilbees roll out the leaf maps at the incline of the branch. Those who witnessed the deaths of those unfortunate bees who perished in the apple sauce were in fear, those new-bees that were healthy were excited, and those that were wounded were hopeful.

"Attention!" The call by a Councilbee silenced most of the crowd. We looked up and saw Meadowlark standing beside the two maps.

"Before we begin educating you new-bees, you all must know that each and every one of you will be responsible for educating every single new-bee that joins our great tree. These truths must be known by all the bees in this land that wish to be free. Now let us begin."

Many of the bees leaned in to see the maps that confused everyone at first, including me when I first saw them. Meadowlark began going over the basics just to make sure that everyone was clear.

"My name is Meadowlark and the Grand Oak is as much *my* home as it is *yours*. These twelve bees that stand beside me are Members of the Grand Oak Council that represent the bees of this tree. These honorable Councilbees also serve as Commanders for the twelve Companies that defend and protect this great tree. You new-bees should know that these twelve Companies were your liberators."

I then thought of the warriors and looked down to the split-branch to see them and realized that they were not there! Nervously I looked around and was relieved to see that they were standing together with the crowd listening to Meadowlark. It appeared that they had learned their lesson.

"Your sisters here have liberated you from your box-hive and from the mistakes made by your warriors. The warriors have decided to join us in our liberation force and they should be forgiven by all bees regardless of what they have done. Let all the bees here know that the Grand Oak is a forgiving place that has the power to purify creatures of their wrongdoings." A few bees noticed the warriors as I did and looked at them seriously. Though the new-bees that were harmed by the warriors had no desire to forgive them at the moment, they knew that in time this would all pass. We all were bees and soon we would all know our common goal.

"So, just to inform you, the structure that you have been living in for all of your lives, we refer to as a box-hive. This box-hive that you call the Meridian Hive is in fact a fake wooden hive made by a giant devilish creature named Oersted who built these boxes on this land to reap in massive amounts of your precious honey. You have all been raised to believe that all of your honey goes into storage cells in the hive, when in reality, there is a terrible monster exploiting and depleting your honey reserves. Oersted is the most evil creature that has ever walked this earth. I hate this devil just as much as the free-bees of this tree do—revenge is what we seek and revenge is what we'll get."

The audience was stunned. The enthusiasm in the new-bees sparked from this knowledge earned them a higher level of respect among the free-bees. Meadowlark scanned the crowd.

"Are you all with me so far? Are there any questions?" The new-bees obviously had questions but no one was bold enough to ask so Meadowlark simply continued. "Alright then, as you can see by these maps, the entire farm where Oersted conducts his business is laid out."

I had heard all of this before but it was still enjoyable to watch the other new-bees learn as I did. Most of them paid close attention to Meadowlark as he explained the maps and the different areas of the farm. During the educational assembly, I realized that I was in a tight and otherwise uncomfortable spot in the crowd. Though I physically sat uncomfortably, I was content with where I was because of what was being said and how my sisters were listening.

Smiling, I looked around at the entire crowd and the faces of my compatriots. Then I noticed Harriet sitting with a group of bees that I had not seen before. She sat with several other older bees in a semicircle at the back of the crowd facing Meadowlark. In her little cluster with her colleagues, she and the others were scribbling on pieces of leaves with their stingers. It appeared as if they were documenting everything that came out of Meadowlark's beak and putting it on the leaves.

The assembly continued into the afternoon as many came and went. Most of the audience stayed seated for the entire duration of the meeting while some grabbed some honey to eat and came back. With all of this education filling the minds of the new-bees, they began to join the collective of the free-bees and started to abandon the title of 'new-bee' in the tree. After the long seminar by Meadowlark, he yielded the floor to the Councilbees to inform all of the bees what tomorrow's mission would look like.

"For those of you who do not know me, I am Councilbee Rosa. Let us now go over the logistics of tomorrow's mission. As we have made it clear to you all, our mission is to free the rest of the box-hives from Oersted's clutches. Our next objective is the Luna Hive. Assuming that there is no militant resistance there to outsiders, we will assume the role of peaceful educators and pass through the box-hive to wake up each and every bee there. As you probably all know, the young Queen Luna is a celebrated and beloved leader that rules the hive. If we can gain her attention and support, perhaps we can turn the tide of the entire box-hive, educate them all, and free them from their prison when the time is right. We need to be careful now because we have increased numbers and will be infiltrating another hive. We must always keep an eye out for

Oersted who now knows that something is up." Meadowlark stepped forward and added to Rosa's briefing.

"And take note that no bee should be hostile to any other fellow bee regardless of their bondage status. You all must remain peaceful and educational to them. You must show them what freedom is." Many bees in the crowd nodded at this statement.

"Our plan is simple. Peace is our goal with our sisters below so that they may also join our glorious cause. Trust in your Commanders' leadership and be ready to inform your fellow bees. Tomorrow we will distribute leaf pamphlets that have been dipped in our sweet Grand Oak honey to all the Luna bees. They will not only be able to read what we have here but they will also be able to taste it." All the bees smiled at the brilliant idea. Then Harriet stood up from her group and attracted the attention of the bees to the back of the High Branch where she was standing.

"This is all well and good but because of this project and the new addition to our tree, we require more nectar for ourselves and for our future Luna sisters. So please join us in our nectar gathering afternoon and know that all of it is yours—there will be no tolls, and by the power of the Grand Oak no bee will go hungry tonight." The crowd cheered at this and began to disperse and prepare to forage for the nectar. The bees shoddily began to disperse from the assembly as the increased populace somehow decreased the amount of control the Council held over them. But Meadowlark held them together.

"Halt, sisters!" All the bees stopped in their tracks and looked at Meadowlark. "The meeting must be adjourned properly with our unanimous gratitude to our great home. Now all of you echo this supplication: Oak be praised!"

"*Oak be praised!*" The sound was large and united. The common prayer was upheld and the Grand Oak was respected. This gave the Council more authority and admiration because of Meadowlark. Finally, the crowd was allowed to disassemble.

I walked with Harriet and many other bees over to one side of the High Branch where we would launch to go on our gathering-flight. We looked down out of the tree and looked in the distance where Harriet began pointing.

"For you new-bees, get ready to taste the sweetness of pine."

"Pine? What's that?" a new-bee asked.

"Do you see out there where the hills drop off?" We all looked out past the hills. "That is where much of our Grand Oak nectar comes from—pine trees."

"Hey now wait a minute," the same questioning bee said, "That wasn't on the map that Meadowlark showed us." Harriet looked at her with semi-tired eyes.

"We don't need a map to know where to get our nectar. It is impossible to get lost with the guidance of the Grand Oak that stands as a landmark as far as the eye can see. Trust in the Grand Oak and let us go gather that sweet woodland nectar."

"How do we gather pine nectar?" another bee asked.

"Oh my goodness, just have a little faith and let us go!" Harriet took off and all the bees followed her in her flight path. Those who were uncertain still joined in the gathering-flight because they began to have faith in Harriet and the Grand Oak.

As we flew away from the Grand Oak and away from the Oersted Farm, I thought of how beautiful life was with my freedom. I looked around and saw the gorgeous fields of grass waving at us as we flew by. I saw the oak leaves behind me in the tree fluttering in the wind. I became so dazed by the beauty that I nearly knocked into another bee in the gathering-flight's formation.

We reached the end of the short hills and saw the pine trees. They were tall, skinny trees that stood high above the ground but not high enough to dwarf the Grand Oak in size. They were covered in tiny green needles that stuck out at us from the seemingly jagged pinewood branches. This experience was new to me just as it was for the other new-bees but I trusted Harriet and the others enough to not ask too many questions. I wanted to seem experienced.

We landed on a horizontal branch of the first pine tree that we saw and followed Harriet and the other experienced gatherers as they passed through the needles. Most of us were confused and did not understand how we would obtain nectar from the pine tree.

"Harriet, what exactly are we looking for here if there are no flowers?" I asked, seeing that no one else had the urge to ask the question.

"Honeydew. Honeydew, my dear. It doesn't come from flowers, it comes from our local friends the aphids."

"Who?" someone asked.

"The aphids. They are our friends here that produce this honeydew from the sap of this pine tree. The honeydew that they secrete is just another waste product to them that we like to use as nectar in producing our Grand Oak honey." Then Harriet and the others stopped crawling and found many droplets of honeydew in between the needles. "See?" Harriet reached down and drew some honeydew from the droplets onto her tongue. Then the other bees joined her and began collecting the honeydew nectar.

All of this was strange to me. The fact that there were no flowers and that this nectar was being produced supposedly by some other creatures perplexed me. Nevertheless, the gatherers and I filled our sacks with this strange nectar and we were on our merry way to having more honey to support the Grand Oak. But then a droplet splashed down from above near Harriet.

"Well I'll be damned, look who it is boys, its old Harriet!" We looked up and saw a whole herd of small, oval shaped brown creatures that Harriet called the aphids. "Back again to gather that sticky stuff, aye old friend?"

"And just when I thought I'd seen the last of you, Thomas. How have you and the boys been?" Harriet flew up to the branch where they were grazing and sat beside Thomas who was half the size of a honeybee.

"Oh you know, same old same old, business with the wood ants is a little hectic these days but we manage." I flew up behind Harriet and watched them talk after I had already acquired my fill of honeydew.

"If you ever need my help I've got your back; you know Thomas that I'd pull my stinger out for you."

"Well it's not that serious, but I thank you, my friend." Thomas turned over at me. "And who is this young bee with you?"

"My name's Shayla," I said to him with a smile.

"That's a beautiful name. You know I once knew a fire ant with a name like that and man was she hot!" I blushed and laughed at his joyous raunchiness. Then suddenly a giant bronze creature crawled over to Thomas.

"Hey what's going on here, come on Thomas we've got a schedule to keep!" It was one of the wood ants that he was talking about. He glared at Thomas and gave no attention to me or Harriet.

"Yes sir," Thomas said apologetically, walking back to his spot on the branch where he and all of the other aphids were using their long straw-like mouths to suck up the sap from the pine tree. As the wood ant stormed away, Thomas imitated him laughably as Harriet and I tried not to chuckle out loud. He was a kind creature and very friendly. The wood ant eyed us from down the branch and without a word wanted us to leave. So we waved to Thomas and the other aphids and dropped back down to the branch that the gatherers were working on.

"He seems nice," I said to Harriet.

"You can say that again. That little bug has saved my skin more times than I can remember. We became friends from Meadowlark's dream-flights that he would take us on."

"Dream-flights, what are those?"

"Oh just something Meadowlark would do for us back in the day when the Grand Oak only consisted of a few bees and him. He would pile us on his back and he would take us for rides all around the land, farther than we could imagine. It was truly magical…and I got to meet plenty of buggers like Thomas along the way." Harriet smiled and looked up at where he was working.

The idea of a dream-flight with Meadowlark filled my heart and oh how I wished for such a flight. Perhaps one day after this revolution was over my dream-flight with Meadowlark would become a reality. But my realist side doubted that such a thing would ever happen.

The rest of the bees gathered enough honeydew to fill their sacks and prepared for the flight back to the Grand Oak where the sun was already beginning to set. We all leaped out of the pine tree and headed back home over the hills. As we flew through the late afternoon air, I closed my eyes and pretended for a moment that I was flying on Meadowlark's back. For a few moments I could imagine it quite clearly, until I started to pitch downward from the weight of the nectar. My little moment nearly caused me to fall out of the sky, but luckily I shook myself out of it and flapped my wings madly to compensate. Harriet noticed my strangeness and flew close to me.

"Someday kid, someday." I cheerfully smiled. We all returned to the Grand Oak and landed on the Long Branch. Some new hives were nearly finished and bees were already moving in for the night. We needed to drop off our nectar to be processed at the larger hive that served as a Dining Hall. Inside, bees were constantly being served honey but also in the corners there were others processing nectar and filling honeycombs. We walked in and each found a partner to extract the nectar and all went smoothly. In a matter of moments we were all done and it was time for us to go our separate ways in the Grand Oak for the night.

I stepped out of the Dining Hall hive and looked around to find the hive where Harriet and I had left Rae. I waited for Harriet to finish passing out her nectar and then we both walked over to check on Rae. Harriet led the way to the small hive and we both stopped at the entrance. We looked inside and saw no one. Rae must have gotten up and gone. We entered the hive and saw no sign of her anywhere inside. Harriet and I figured that she must have been alright and just walked out to join the public. Most likely, if she was not working, she was probably reclining in a newly built hive.

All was well, and we left the hive to go our separate ways. But before we parted I had to ask Harriet about tomorrow's mission.

"Harriet, why haven't we been called by our Company Commanders down to the barracks?"

"That's because tomorrow's mission will not be a military mission but rather a diplomatic one. We cannot

112

seem threatening like we did before to the warriors. We must be able to scatter and spread this information while the Councilbees confront Queen Luna. So find a hive to sleep in, and I will see you in the morning." We both tipped our antennae at each other and said adieu.

Harriet flew away as I looked around for a place to sleep for the night. I knew just the place. I first went back to the Dining Hall and picked up a bit of honey. Then I came out and crawled to a medium sized hive next to a side-branch. I looked inside and saw just what I wanted to see: my three best friends lying in their cribs talking and joking with each other. I entered the hive.

"A little delivery, girls," I said upon my entrance. They turned to me and saw the honey in my hands.

"Hey Shayla, c'mon in!" Elizabeth welcomed me. I walked into the hive and sat down in the middle where the girls sat up in their cribs. "Say, that's some fine looking gold, my sister." They all eyed the honey.

"Yeah, I scraped some from the newest batch, here have some." They all got out of their cribs and sat with me on the floor where I placed the honey. They all thanked me and sat in a circle with me reclining on the floor of the hive.

"So how did the gathering go?" Anne asked me.

"It was fun, I got to meet some other creatures out in the pine tree. But I have to ask; over the hill I saw hundreds of these pine trees, why are there so many, what is that place?"

"You mean the forest, where there is no end in sight."

113

"Do you mean that it goes on forever?" Anne thought about it for a moment, looked at the other girls, and then back at me.

"Well, I'd say so, but no one has really gone far enough to know for sure. Over those hills is a whole other world." I imagined the true size of the forest as we all sipped the fresh golden honey. I was just starting to know freedom and I could nearly imagine the scale of the pine forest. Then Elizabeth came closer to me.

"Shayla, you can obviously live here with us in this hive. As Meadowlark would say; this is as much *my* hive as it is *yours*." Elizabeth made us laugh from her spot-on Meadowlark impression.

"Oh for crying out loud, stop it Elizabeth!" I said laughing. "But thank you very much for letting me stay girls."

"But there is one catch, Shayla," Elizabeth said.

"And what's that?"

"You're coming with us tomorrow during the mission."

"Gladly," I said with a winsome smile. "I wouldn't have it any other way." We proceeded to finish the sample of honey, then crawled into our cribs and fell asleep.

THE SUN ROSE TO ANNOUNCE ANOTHER DAY OF REVOLU-
tion as we awoke to the pleasant morning air. I got up
out of my crib and looked around. Naturally, the girls
were already up-and-at-'em. I came out of the hive and
saw that they were standing next to a huge pile of leaf
pamphlets dripping with honey. They began to separate
the pile into smaller stacks as I approached to help
them.

"Morning Shayla," said Elizabeth who grabbed a
stack of pamphlets. "Here, take these." I took the
pamphlets from Elizabeth and felt the gooey honey
dripping down off of my hands. If this isn't the most
delicious read in the world, I don't know what is, I
thought. It looked like about fifty pamphlets that I realized had a different language on them. Instead of the
complex characters of the *Oak Leaf*, these pamphlets
were covered with simple drawings and interpretations
of the large leaf maps of the Council. The sketches de-
picted scenes and basic explanations of the box-hive
bees' enslavement. Elizabeth noticed how I was looking at the writing.

"It's good, isn't it?"

"Yeah, I mean, even *I* can understand it," I said.

"Well *that's* the idea." Elizabeth picked up her stack of pamphlets and motioned for us all to start walking. "Let's go girls, there's no time to waste."

Emily had her pamphlets in hand and began to follow Elizabeth. I was about to join her but I saw Anne struggling with her stack—it looked like she was about to drop it. I rushed over and saved her from dropping the leaves. She got a grip on the stack, stood up, thanked me, and then we began walking together. We walked along the Long Branch where bees were just starting to wake up.

Down the branch we could see Meadowlark standing upright in his nest with the twelve Councilbees staring at the Luna Hive below. Their statures were quite noble as they prepared themselves for their confrontation with Queen Luna herself. Their mission was by far more important than our menial task of posting pamphlets about and talking to bees that would just write us off as savages unless Queen Luna herself had accepted us. Gaining such an acceptance relied solely on Meadowlark and the Council, I thought.

The girls and I were excited to the point that we had no desire to wait for any other group of bees to fly down to the box-hive. The strictness for the timing of this mission was rather pliant because the Council decided that it would seem too hostile if our masses were to organize into lines and companies—that type of tyranny of *forcing* knowledge down bees' throats was certainly not the message of the Grand Oak.

As we looked down at the Luna Hive we could see that some of our bees had already left to start the mission. This mission appeared to be less stirring than the last one and more menial of a task, yet it was equally as vital to our cause. Looking down and squinting I assumed that Harriet was among the first of the bees to go down. After all, she is probably the most involved bee I know around here. In this peaceful mission, I would not be surprised to see her taking the lead. The girls and I stood at the edge of the Long Branch, ready to jump.

"Well…shall we?" Elizabeth leaped off of the branch first with the three of us following after her jump. We spiraled to the ground, flapping our wings to compensate for the weight of the pamphlets. We each hit the dirt around the Grand Oak in sequence and looked at each other to make sure everyone was alright. I'll admit it, they all looked at me to make sure I did not break my legs on the drop—this subtle attention came as the price for pursuing my deepest callings and for being a new-bee in the tree.

We began to walk through the tall grass blades with our heavy loads. The hot sun combined with the humidity of the grass encumbered us with much burden as we lugged the hefty honey-laced stacks through the field. As we walked to fulfill the mission, ironically we felt like slaves ourselves bringing knowledge to *real* slaves that would set them free.

Sweaty, the girls and I emerged from the field of grass onto the dirt at the foot of the bush line that encased the box-hive prison zone. Because it was just the four of us, we decided to weave ourselves through the dense bushes to get to the other side. Pushing through the tight passageway we managed to emerge onto the other side with our heavy stacks of pamphlets intact for the most part.

From where we entered into the prison zone, the Meridian Hive was the first landmark that presented itself to us. The box-hive stood still and dreary with no activity in or around its wooden walls. As we walked past my former home, I looked up to see the apple sauce dish hanging slightly off the edge of the roof. At the rim of the dish I could see the stiff arms of the dead bees who were captured by the trap. Oersted initiated their deaths by utilizing the selfish nature of slave-bees to bring them back to prison.

When Oersted finds the box-hive still empty with only the few dead bees in the dish, I pondered, he will be just as dissatisfied as we were that the bees died on their way back to the box-hive. Oersted wanted to re-populate the prison with his trap while we wanted to save those bees from dying, but in the end, death resolved that neither side was victorious.

Their deaths only added to the casualties that were sustained during the liberation. Not that the bees were harmed on the way to the Grand Oak, but rather that many succumbed to starvation and or wounds sustained from box-hive brawls. Much of the branches in the Grand Oak had become infirmaries that I could not imagine saved *every* single dying bee. Not to mention the casualties sustained by the Meridian bees after the wasp raid. In short, lives had been lost in the midst of the revolution but not for its cause—the pity was too great to dwell on, I had to stay on task.

After passing the Meridian Hive, the Luna Hive came into view. Its populous was visibly lively on the outside where nectar gathering and hive renovations were taking place. Seeing how the bees flew around and worked together, it did not appear that they had any desire of abandoning their home. The closer we came to the box-hive, the more I thought of how vital the Council's meeting with Queen Luna would be to gaining the support of the Luna bees.

We came to the foot of the box-hive where the Luna Public Porch was situated and paused for a minute. Our recollection of the welcome we received before at the Meridian Hive caused us to hesitate and look around for warriors that would want to stop us. But none of the warriors we saw looked at us with disdain or malice. Instead they looked at us smiling and shaking their heads, thinking, "Oh no, not another one of these outcast preachers."

Nevertheless, we started to walk into the hive with our stacks of pamphlets and noticed that some bees of ours were already posting pamphlets against the wooden walls, attaching them with the adhesiveness of the honey. Inside, the Luna Hive was well-lit by its golden honeycomb reserves that were just as plentiful if not more plentiful than that of the Grand Oak reserves. Hunger was not an issue for the Luna Hive bees nor was there any indication of open oppression from the warriors.

We looked around for a place to start handing out our pamphlets and thought it convenient to hand them out at the entrance where bees were coming and going at will. We proceeded to stand apart from each other at the entrance, stacks at our sides, trying to hand out pamphlets to those who entered or exited the hive. At first no bee paid any attention to us. The only attention we received was from the entrance guard-warriors who watched as we desperately held out the leaves.

When bees would pass by, we each buzzed quickly to explain everything about the Grand Oak in one condensed statement that could not be finished in time before the bees flew away. The lack of retort from the passing bees frustrated each of us. I then looked over at the bees that were pasting the pamphlets to the walls. I walked over to one of them.

"Excuse me sister, why are you stamping the pamphlets against the walls? Aren't we supposed to be educating bees ourselves?" She looked at me with an equally frustrated expression.

"Sister, if personal educating is what you want to do, be my guest, but after trying that for some time myself, I find that bees don't want to be *told* the truth by some other bee. Perhaps it would be better for them to stumble upon it themselves against these here walls, don't you think?" I pondered this concept.

"You might be onto something, comrade," I said with my head tilted, examining her long line of posted pamphlets. I turned around and beckoned to the three girls who came to me with haste. As soon as they came close I turned to the lone bee. "Do you mind if we join you?"

"Not at all," she said as we began pasting our sticky pamphlets to the walls nearby. We placed a few to the wall before the bee turned around and spoke again. "You know, those walls over there are looking pretty empty, why don't you girls spread out so we can cover more territory." The bee smiled.

We began walking around to the bare wooden walls and began to paste our pamphlets there as well. I looked back at the lone bee that we had just conversed with. She looked much older than us, perhaps nearly Harriet's age—she appeared to be a true freedom fighter, dedicated, and calm.

I then glanced at the warriors at the entrance who saw that we were making progress. Their snickering smiles disappeared and they looked around at the few Luna Bees who began to gaze at our pamphlets. I looked at the passing bees that stumbled upon the leaf-fliers as they slowed to a stop and read. It appeared that the simplified drawings and lack of complex language led many bees to comprehend the pamphlets. Upon understanding the posts, some bees continued to walk without a real care for what was said while others read and reread fixatedly.

As this was going on, more bees from the Grand Oak began to arrive. The girls and I had finished pasting most of our pamphlets against the wall, seeing as that was becoming the most efficient way to get this information out. I looked to the outside of the hive and was pleased to see nearly the entire Grand Oak parading en masse. Many of our sisters passed through the entrance, paying little attention to the guard warriors who had dropped jaws and raised brows at the surprising enormity of our following.

The girls and I took our few remaining pamphlets and began walking near the incoming mob of bees. Many had smiles across their faces with pamphlets in their hands. Others came without any of the leaves; just with their living bodies that visually supported our cause. We saw that a large conglomeration of the parade was mainly former Meridian bees who had been freed by the grace of the Grand Oak. They gathered at the inner base of the hive where we had been posting our pamphlets. Then two bees placed their stacks of pamphlets in the center of the inner hive and one bee stood up on top of the stacks.

"Dear bees, won't you listen to a word of truth on this bright and beautiful day?" said the former Meridian bee who stood as an educated and truly open-minded individual who had the ability to perceive the vision of the Grand Oak. It appeared that this bee had woken up to the truth much quicker than I did on arrival to the Grand Oak. I envied her slightly because of this and wished that I could have adapted to the freedom lifestyle and ideology as quickly as she appeared to do so in a very short time. Perhaps the reward of sudden freedom after sudden oppression was enough to open the mind of this bee.

"I am Margret and I am a freed bee. I stand before you as a humble bee who has known slavery long enough to finally see that living in freedom is a most virtuous life. My sisters and I who have managed to escape from the Meridian Hive have been granted freedom for already one whole day and one whole night in the great Grand Oak that towers above this awful prison land."

Her words were eloquent and spoken with a wide smile that had a subtle nuance of nervousness. Many bees passing by in the Luna Hive stopped to listen to her and to see the large crowd that was piling into the box-hive from the Public Porch. As Margret talked to the public at the bottom of the hive, many began to observe and analyze the pamphlets on the walls as well as her boldness to stand on those stacks of leaves, but to some Luna bees, she looked like a fool.

She took a more daring stance on the stack of leaves. "The truth, my sisters, is that this hive is a *prison*. You work to make honey that ends up in the mouth of a demon that embezzles it from you. Here you have no freedom in this mockery of a true hive. Your home truly belongs in the Grand Oak, away from this place, high above the—" She suddenly tripped off of the stack of pamphlets as she attempted to stand higher on them. She fell to the ground, igniting the laughter of many bees in the hive while her comrades nearby rushed to help her back to her feet.

The pamphlets from the tall stacks flipped into the air and began to land all over the bees in the middle of the floor, especially all over Margret. They stuck to her body, wet and dripping with honey. Margret had a pitiful frown on her face as her compatriots removed the sticky pamphlets from her body. It was hard to find one Luna bee that was not laughing at her. One of Margret's friends looked up at the laughing crowd and spoke angrily.

"What my sister says is true!" The statement was muffled by the laughter and commotion as bees began to leave the crowd. I was so infuriated from the present situation that I started to move toward the center of the room where all of the fallen pamphlets laid stuck to the ground. Elizabeth and the other girls saw how exasperated I was and tried to stop me but I marched too quickly for them to hinder my bold move. I lifted the last pamphlet off of Margret and held it high in the air.

"The next bee that laughs is going to get this leaf rammed down their throat!" I shouted. Every bee looked at me. The laughter stopped as I stood there scanning the faces of the Luna bees circled around the scene. Many looked at me in fear. I then realized that my stinger was drawn.

Looking around I saw that many had stopped to stare at me. The girls looked at me with wide eyes, wishing for me to stop this imprudently intrepid act. Without shouting another word, a few Luna bees began to pick the pamphlets off of the ground where they were scattered. Many saw this and began to humbly lift the leaves off the ground as well, fetching the pamphlets up to read. My stinger was holstered and I lowered the pamphlet that I held high down to my side.

As bees were beginning to read the pamphlets, some warriors snaked through the crowd into the open where I and the other free-bees were standing. They observed that their fellow Luna bees were curiously examining the pamphlets and then looked at me standing slightly apart from my comrades. They approached me authoritatively.

"Is this the bee that has drawn her stinger inside of our public commons?!" They pointed at me with their larger stingers drawn. I stood angrily, ready to draw my stinger again if need be.

"We come in peace," said Margret coming close to me. She held my hand and stood beside me passionately. "She meant no harm!"

Margret was shoved away by the leading warrior. The warriors quickly surrounded me and lifted me off the ground. They held me by my wings so I could not escape—I was in big trouble.

The three warriors that persisted in holding me restrained carried me out of the crowd and away from the commotion. As we left, I could hear my fellow comrades arguing for my release, while my legs swung back and forth trying to escape but with no great success. Shouting for them to release me was futile—it was time for me to be taken where the troublesome bees go, wherever that might be.

They carried me tightly up the hive, across many sheets of honeycomb and passing bees. I glanced at the Luna bees who gave me disdainful looks as I passed. I despised their unspoken opinions of me and looked with hatred to their slavish facilities. I thought it curious that in trying to liberate them, I had in fact threatened them.

We arrived at a precipice in the hive where there were many guard-warriors waiting. They carried me into this heavily guarded room and dropped me on the ground. When I got up I was surprised to see that I was in the midst of Queen Luna and her servants standing across a table from Harriet and a few of her close colleagues. It appeared that they had been in conversation before my arrival interrupted their exchange. They all looked at me strangely as my brows raised. The warriors who had dropped me turned to the Queen.

"My Queen, this insolent *savage* has caused a disturbance below during this peculiar parade; it is our desire to make an example of her in front of the savages below to deport them from our hive, your majesty." Queen Luna, with her youthfully gorgeous face looked at the warrior and started to speak.

"To the best of my knowledge, *I*, the sovereign Queen of this hive, make the decisions. Is that not clear, warrior? Do you perhaps wish to act against our guests with unwarranted force?" The Queen's words were surprising and strong. I looked up at the warrior who was stunned.

"No your graciousness, pardon me, my Queen." Queen Luna looked at her seriously and turned to Harriet and the other bees who were diplomatically standing impartial to the present situation. The Queen turned back to the subservient warrior.

"I will have you know that the honorable Ms. Harriet and I are in the middle of a pleasant discussion. Will you not leave us to our pleasantries?" The warriors readied themselves to leave with their arms again wrapped around me.

"My Queen, we will respectfully leave your majesty, but what are we to do with this bee that we have brought you?"

"If you have brought her to me, then leave her in our midst and exit my chamber at once!" The warriors quickly released their grip on my arms and let me go. They obediently departed from the Queen's chamber and disappeared. I was left there on my knees, looking at the bees that sat around the table glaring at me. Queen Luna however had no desire to scowl at me; rather, she preferred to smile.

"Well for goodness sake dear, stand up and sit among your sisters." I stood up slowly, showing respect to her, for I realized that she had just saved my life from certain demise. Those warriors would have beaten me to death and hung my dead body up against the walls where our pamphlets had been posted. I slowly approached Harriet and her associates who made space for me to sit beside them. The diplomatic discussion finally continued.

"Regarding this meeting that we seek to arrange, your Majesty, our leader would like to converse with you in the patch of grass beside the bush line that surrounds this area." Harriet apparently was collaborating with Queen Luna to organize a meeting with Meadowlark, the Council, and the Queen away from the Luna Hive.

"Hmm, and would there be a particular reason why this privacy is necessary for this meeting with your leader?" the Queen asked Harriet.

"Our leader prefers to speak with your Majesty in private considering the possible immense upheaval of disruption the public may pose. He feels that to fully respect her Majesty, he must allow this meeting to be mutual and uninterrupted." Queen Luna's face turned a different emotion than thankfulness for the consideration.

"Does this leader of yours think that I am incapable of handling the public opinion of my loyal bees? I will have you know that my daughters know my strength and will follow me to the end of the earth if I choose to venture there. I have no fear of my own bees. Tell your leader that if we shall meet, we shall meet on the balcony of my own hive, on my terms. Is this understood Ms. Harriet?" Queen Luna's arrogance was becoming clear to me just as it was to Harriet and the rest of the diplomats from the Grand Oak. Even young Queen Luna's personal subordinates knew well of her haughtiness.

"Yes your Majesty, on behalf of the Grand Oak, we agree to your honorable terms. Shall we schedule this encounter on the roof of this hive to be at sunset, your Majesty?" It appeared that Harriet was still trying to arrange a meeting where the public would not interfere with the affairs of the Queen and Meadowlark. Perhaps Harriet also took into consideration the fear that the Luna bees might experience upon seeing Meadowlark's colossal form.

"No my friend, I say you shall return to your leader, inform him of my decision and arrive at the peak of my kingdom *with haste*. Let us settle this issue plainly and speedily, in front of *all* of my daughters to see." Harriet looked at her subordinates and me and then back at the Queen.

"It shall be done, your Majesty. Thank you, your Graciousness, for allowing us this consultation." All of the Grand Oak bees in the room stood up as I quickly rose to my feet to follow them. We all bowed to Queen Luna and began to follow Harriet out of the room. Before we totally left the room I looked back at Queen Luna. She stood there motionless with her chin up, beautifully thinking and preparing her own self for the imminent meeting that she had just arranged.

Outside of the royal chamber we all stood for a moment and Harriet looked at me. "Shayla, is that true, what the warriors said you did?"

I said, "Yes." She came closer to me so that the guards outside of the chamber could not hear.

"I'm proud of you my dear," she whispered, "but this situation here is very delicate with this *pompous* Queen we have to deal with while maintaining a good relationship with these Luna bees. Save that kind of energy for the *real* fight, do you understand?"

"Yes ma'am." We began walking slowly down out of the hive to the Public Porch. We passed the enormous crowd at the base of the hive where apparently bees were reading the pamphlets en masse and all was well. Luckily there was much conversation between the Luna bees and the free-bees that sparked friendships and understanding between our two groups. On the Public Porch the other bees that accompanied Harriet flew off to go inform Meadowlark while Harriet waited for a moment to talk to me.

"Shayla, this meeting is of crucial importance to the destiny of these bees—find your sisters and ready them for this public meeting. We must remain peaceful at all times while asserting ourselves to these box-dwellers. In this situation we must trust the judgment of Meadowlark and the Councilbees and be prepared to take action on their accord. Now go, tell your sisters!" Harriet flew out of sight back to the Grand Oak.

I turned around and quickly returned to the box-hive. I looked around through the crowd for my friends. As I shifted myself through the tight crowd and avid conversations, I finally found my three friends talking with Margret and her friends. Shoving myself over to them, they saw me and rushed over.

"Oak be praised, you're alive!" said Emily.

"I admit I made a mistake but there's no time to talk about that now," I babbled rapidly, "we need to tell *every* bee here that Meadowlark and the Council will be meeting with Queen Luna herself at the top of this hive in only a few moments. Quick! Tell everyone!"

They looked at me strangely for a second and then fanned out into the crowd, shouting the news. Bees ceased their conversations and listened closely. I did not want to yell the news and draw attention to myself again, afraid that I might cause another disturbance. Nevertheless, the bees at the base of the hive became informed of this announcement and soon bees began to exit the hive onto the Public Porch to look up at the roof of the hive. They saw no bees on the roof at the moment but knew that soon this meeting would commence.

I came outside with the crowd and leaped into the air, as many did, to get a better view of the white wooden roof. Then out of the crease came several guards surrounding the young Queen Luna. She walked proudly onto the roof as thunderous applause for her began. Many of us hovered in the air around the roof, clapping our wings together. From behind me came my three friends, accompanied by Margret and her friends who flew close to me. Margret quickly introduced me to each of her two friends.

"Lynnette, Kim—Shayla, Shayla—Lynnette and Kim."

"How do you do."

"It's a pleasure to meet you, Shayla, let's talk after, this is far too important to miss." We turned back to look at the stage of the roof surrounded by a massive circle of hovering bees.

"Isn't that the truth," I said grinning. We hovered there for a while watching Queen Luna stand with her associates who had formed themselves into a line behind her as she faced the direction of the Grand Oak. Then all of the twelve Councilbees came out of the blue sky and hovered above the wooden roof examining the crowd. There was applause from the free-bees but little from the Luna bees; only curious stares.

The twelve-member Council landed at once and organized into a formal line in front of the Queen, bowing courteously. As soon as they all rose to make eye contact with the Queen she had stepped forward with her hands behind her back.

"And which one of you bees might be the leader who desires to meet with me?" she said looking down upon the twelve bees from her slightly taller stature above. None of them spoke. They stood there expressionless looking at the Queen. She squinted at all of them back and forth in the line. Queen Luna was about to speak before being interrupted by a huge gust that pushed nearly every bee out of the air and almost toppled the Queen and her followers. It was Meadowlark swooping in. He landed in front of the Councilbees who stepped back to make room for his substantial size. Queen Luna was stunned, looking up at him with her jaw on the ground. The hovering audience stabilized itself after Meadowlark's wing flapping had ceased and looked on intensely.

"I am their leader, Meadowlark of the Grand Oak!" The impact of his deep voice pierced much of the audience and stunned Queen Luna. The applause from the free-bees became earsplitting. The Queen stood up to him in a dynamic stance while Meadowlark folded his wings.

"Are you a bee-eater bird, who feasts on honeybee flesh?!" inquired Queen Luna seriously. The warriors behind her readied their stingers while many in the audience gasped.

"If I was, would not the bees behind me be in my belly rather than at my side?" Meadowlark made it clear that he was no bee-eater and that, assuming his stance, he had no stomach for the diplomatic vernacular of referring to the Queen as *her Majesty*. Since he was not a bee-eater, he clearly displayed his abilities of leadership and strength around the bees that supported him and those who were yet to sympathize with him and this cause.

The warriors put away their stingers as Queen Luna instructed and backed up. The Queen came near to Meadowlark, taking a seemingly firm stance in front of him.

"Acknowledging you as their leader for the moment, what have you come to discuss here on this public stage?" Meadowlark looked around at the ring of hovering bees watching them.

"We have come to inform you of the truth about your lives."

"And what would that be."

"That you are slaves." Queen Luna, expecting an expression of disgust from the audience, was disappointed to hear silence from her daughters who were already well-read on the circulated pamphlets; they knew well enough what Meadowlark was talking about. "And the other news we bring you is that we can set you free."

"Free from what?" asked the Queen.

"Free from the tyranny of the gargantuan demon, larger than I, who exploits your resources at will. You know as well as I do that we are standing on a honey-filled, comb-capped hive. Very soon, the demon I speak of will arrive and exploit nearly all of your honey from your hive, forcing your daughters to work harder than they have to, becoming soulless creatures, slaves to their toils."

"If this is true, then why can't we see this demon you speak of?"

"He is invisible to you because he sprays you all with gas to blind and sedate you! *That's* when he steals from you! We want to save your livelihoods and invite you to join us in our cause against this monster. We can offer you a greater home in the Grand Oak where you will be safe and protected from this prison that you have been born in." Meadowlark's words offended Queen Luna to a degree, but deep down, in a way, she knew he was speaking the truth.

"This honey," the Queen spoke in a near whisper, "that uh, is beneath our feet, might there be some way to save it from being stolen by this demon?"

"But of course! If you and your colony would aid us, we are prepared to lift each and every honeycomb sheet of your hive up to the Grand Oak where you can live and enjoy your riches. However, there are two conditions; you must first agree to join us in our home of the Grand Oak, and second, you must extract your honey from the wooden sheets and dispose of the frames that hold them."

"Why is this necessary?"

"In order to know *true freedom*, you must abandon your old way of housing honey and embrace the natural methods provided by the Grand Oak." Meadowlark saw that she did not fully comprehend him. "With experience, you will understand freedom as we do." Then the Queen turned to her fellow bees hovering around the roof.

"My daughters, I know well the great lengths you are willing to take to venture where I fly. My very scent draws you to obey me and follow me wherever I go. But now faced with a drastic change that will alter the lives of every bee in this hive, I must ask my daughters where they wish to go. What say ye?"

"Wait!" Andrea cried from behind Meadowlark, "Before a decision is made, will you bees not look at what this demon has done to your cousin bees over at the Meridian Hive? In an attempt to keep them at their prison, this demon placed a trap that now contains several of their lifeless corpses—look!" Nearly every bee in the circle and on the roof looked over a ways away to see the Meridian Hive with the apple sauce dish still standing on its roof. The bodies of the Meridian bees that could not handle freedom lay all around the bowl, consumed by the snare of deception.

The Luna bees turned back to the roof with horror hanging from their faces. Queen Luna also saw the silent carnage of the Meridian Hive that they all have been reluctant to recognize as of late. Then, seeing how the Luna bees were silent and scared, the free-bees in the crowd hovering next to their Luna sisters began to chant softly: "freedom, freedom, freedom, freedom." As the chant continued, gradually getting louder and louder, the Luna bees began to chime in, matching their voices to the suggestion of the free-bees.

"Freedom, freedom, freedom!" they all chanted at a rhythmic pace. Meadowlark looked around nodding his head at the chanting.

"And where does this freedom preside?!" yelled Meadowlark. In response all of the free-bees knew exactly where.

"O. A. K. Oak! O. A. K. Oak!" they crooned loudly. The Luna bees soon caught onto this chant and joined in the singing. Queen Luna looked around seriously, examining those who chanted and realized that the majority of her hive had spoken.

"Very well!" the Queen said strongly, "Open the lid and let us go forth and beyond this place to this *freedom* that you desire!" Instantly, the circle of hovering bees became a square formation that flew down to grab a side of the wooden lid on the roof. We all heaved but could not lift it. We realized that the stone block was not removed yet. Then Meadowlark with all his might grasped the stone block with his claws and powerfully flung it off of the hive. At the very moment it left the surface of the roof, the lid was completely lifted off of the box-hive and thrown to the side as well.

Looking down from above, many of the bees had never seen the hive like this before. The entire layout of the box-hive was exposed and it became clear that this truly was a prison to the bees. The wooden honeycomb sheets then became covered with all of us, pulling the honey-rich frames out of the box and lifting them into the air. The Councilbees spread out to the floating sheets and guided us all to the Grand Oak swiftly before we could cease chanting or run out of energy. Meadowlark stayed back for a moment to replace the lid and the block on the top of the box to make it seem as if this great robbery had never occurred.

We all reached the tree with the ten extremely heavy honeycomb frames. Each of the laboring groups hinged the frames between creases in the Grand Oak where new branches shot out off of the main trunk. Somehow we had done it! The Luna bees had joined us already, the free-bees were never more potent, and Queen Luna had finally made a decision that was in accordance with the bees that she governed. Perhaps her leadership would conflict with Meadowlark's, I thought, but as I looked at how she conversed with the Councilbees on the way up to the tree, I could already foresee her destiny with the Grand Oak—we needed her, whether we liked to admit it or not.

JUST AS MEADOWLARK INSTRUCTED, WE STARTED TO CUT the honeycombs out of the wooden frames. It was a tedious task, requiring the use of our teeth and much neatness. We trimmed large pieces off of the frames and then transported them away to different parts of the Grand Oak where we had already prepared several hives for the new Luna bees to stay. Some of it was also taken to the Dining Hall and ended up feeding many hungry bees of our own.

We found a balance where bees in the tree could share their honey in public within the Dining Hall but also keep private honey for themselves in their own hives. The system worked well when honey levels were high and when they were low, we would feel the repercussions but never to the extent that the damage was catastrophic. Our economy only worked well because there was no massive taxation levied by Oersted. But I feared that our greater numbers now in conjunction with the fact that there are two completely desolate box-hives below would make us a bigger target for Oersted and we might very well be discovered.

I looked around at the Grand Oak where bees were busy all around. The former Meridian new-bees helped the Luna new-bees adjust into their new homes. The hives were freshly built, hanging off of many branches of the tree. Taking a gander at the totality of the Grand Oak, I estimated our numbers to be in the thousands. I was proud to be a part of this society and was genuinely pleased to serve.

After cutting the last of the honey out of the frames and dispatching it to the new hives, most of us were relieved of our duties for the day, to enjoy the freedom granted by the Grand Oak. Many felt the need to gather more resources from the pine forest, presumably led by Harriet. She seemed to be the busiest of all of us bees, working day-in and day-out behind the scenes. I had enough stress and anxiety from the day that I desired nothing more than to see my friends and meet my new acquaintances.

I flew around for a while through the sea of buzzing bees looking for my friends who had always seemed to depart from me whenever large maneuvers took place. Logically I found them by the side-branch off of the Long Branch where they seemed to always monitor the farm. I flew down to the side-branch and hit the wood with a moderate thud. All six of the girls turned around to see me.

"Somebody looks exhausted," Anne said as she caught my eye first.

"Hey," I let out a sigh, "I'm not used to *that* kind of heavy lifting," I smiled.

"I know the feeling," said Margret, "but I'm glad we did *some* heavy lifting rather than *no* lifting at all."

I nodded, just comprehending how lucky we were to gain the support of the Luna bees. Then Elizabeth turned around, without her regular joking smile, but with a mild seriousness that was uncommonly seen in her eyes.

"You know, I can't stand looking down below to see the corpses of the Meridian Hive still stacked in barricades—they each deserve a proper burial."

"And for the bees at the top," Anne added.

"That's right," Elizabeth looked around at each of us and then up and down the Long Branch. "Before we recline, we ought to do something, c'mon, let's get some helping hands." It was at that moment I turned around and saw a large squadron of bees heading out to gather materials from the pine forest. They disappeared into the distance as I stood there with my friends who primed and fluttered their wings.

We walked slowly off of the side-branch onto the Long Branch. Elizabeth led the seven of us along the wood, tapping bees that passed by who knew Elizabeth well. Every single bee that Elizabeth tapped on the shoulder answered her call to action. They all joined our walking cluster and realized the seriousness of the matter even though they were probably just as exhausted as I was after moving the wealth of the Luna Hive.

There were about thirty of us following Elizabeth before she turned around and looked at us. She had a profound expression across her face, unlike anything she had displayed before.

"Let's go make this right…" We all hopped out of the tree and went back to the prison zone. We flew quickly over the bush line and down to the Meridian Hive. When we reached the box-hive, the smell hit us straight on. The stench of the decaying corpses overwhelmed our senses. We stumbled up to the Public Porch of the Meridian Hive where the bees were stacked, sister over sister, about seven bees high all around. Adjusting to the ghastly odor of the dead, we all began to dig in the ground to form a mass grave for the disrespected deceased.

We dug for a long while until finally the hole was at least large enough to fit most of the bodies. The Meridian bees were then lifted out of their morbid stacks and laid down at the center of the grave. Higher and higher, the depression that we had made became filled with the rotting dead. None of us commented during the burial process. All I could think of was Charlie's disgruntled face when I had approached her caring for Rose as she drew her last breaths. Knowing that forgiveness would never be granted from Charlie, I only regretted the fact that I was unable to save Rose. My frustration was put into throwing the dead vigorously onto the pile with my face scrunched in anger.

Sooner or later, Elizabeth realized how I was placing the corpses in the ground and came near. She put her hand on my shoulder to comfort me as I looked up at her. Not a single word was spoken. But I knew I was disrespecting the dead through my own painful regrets. I took a moment to calm down as Elizabeth stood there with me, silent. A single tear ran down my left cheek. I took a deep breath and went back to the business at hand.

A few moments passed. Finally the last body from the barricade was placed gently on the mass grave and we all sighed. But then one of us looked upward at the Meridian Hive's roof which caused the rest to gaze up as well. No one wanted to say it but we all knew that the apple sauce dish still sat firmly on the roof with several dead bodies littered inside it. We all flew up to the dish and landed on the dry rounded edge. All of us were reluctant to get too close to the murky apple sauce below in fear of slipping and drowning into it.

Elizabeth, brave as can be, stepped down into the thick liquid death pit and began to pry the corpses out of the muck. Following in her footsteps, we joined her, dropping the corpses off of the roof upon releasing them from the slime. After the last body was removed, we helped hoist each other out of the dish and flew back down to pick up the bodies. Soon, all of the bodies were in the grave and we began replacing the displaced dirt.

With the top layer of dirt in place, the grave was sealed and we could finally consecrate the dead properly. We stood around the circular mound and bowed our heads. I dipped my face low to the ground and nearly shut my eyes. Then Elizabeth came next to me and tapped my hand.

"Shayla," she whispered smoothly, "would you like to say something?" I turned to her and nodded. Stepping forward I held my hands together.

"These bees," I said softly, "were my sisters. I worked with them, sweat with them, cried with them…fought with them…" I took a brief pause. "My only wish is that they may find peace and freedom somewhere beyond this world. We, and these hallowed grounds, will forever remember their lives and their sacrifices..." then another short pause ensued with my eyes closed, "...Oak be praised..."

"Oak be praised," responded all gently. I stepped back and silence returned to our midst as we held our heads low again. Then suddenly there was a loud whipping sound that shocked us all. We looked up, behind us, where the sound arose. It was the door to Oersted's Lair flinging open! We rushed behind the Meridian Hive, ducking, suddenly afraid.

Out of the structure came Oersted stomping the earth in front of him. After three monstrous steps, he turned around to the open lair. Then out came two other strange creatures, not as tall as the Oersted devil but of the same shape, with long hair that dripped down off of their heads.

"What are they?—"

"Shhh," hissed Elizabeth, "listen!"

We all listened attentively to our front where the three creatures were standing. We were stunned to hear Oersted's voice for the first time. The door shut from the lair as the two small creatures came toward Oersted with linked hands. Oersted spoke deeply and loudly in an incomprehensible tongue. We raised our heads over the low incline of the Public Porch and could see Oersted speaking harshly to the other two creatures that were holding hands.

He was angry. The devil pointed his pale finger at the box-hives in the prison zone and then back at the two smaller beings. Then after much strange yelling, Oersted marched angrily to his shed while the two others stood motionless together. The stomping of Oersted's feet caused us to duck down low and grip the wood.

Then, after rummaging through his demonic shed, Oersted returned with his knife and smoke spray cylinder in hand. Our hearts began to pound faster and faster with great anxiety as Oersted entered the prison zone and began opening the box-hives. He went first to the still-functioning box-hives where their honeycombs were ripe for harvesting. He opened them sequentially with his knife, sprayed the smoke, and then removed the golden honey frames from the boxes.

Before long, we realized that soon the empty Luna Hive would be discovered just as the Meridian Hive was. We had to get out of their fast. Scanning the area for a viable escape, we looked to Elizabeth for leadership. She turned back to the bush line and instructed all of us to fall back and retreat through the bushes toward the Grand Oak. I was terrified of Oersted's close proximity and nervously rushed with the group of bees back to the bush line behind Elizabeth.

Instead of being foolishly obvious, by flying up and over the bushes, we filtered ourselves through the densely packed branches lowest to the ground and made our exit accordingly. Flying swiftly and effectively, we managed to escape and returned to the Grand Oak, shaken with fear. We landed on the Long Branch panting. Some bees near the Dining Hall noticed us and hurried to bring us each a cell of honey to refresh us. We thanked them thoroughly and gladly dined on the honey. They were apparently busy so they returned to the Dining Hall with haste. We sat there for a while, sipping honey and pondering what we had just witnessed.

"Those creatures," I asked again, "what in the world are they?" Elizabeth first looked at the other experienced free-bees, saw that no one could instantaneously articulate the explanation, and then turned back to me.

"Those smaller creatures are Oersted's daughters—"

"You mean he can reproduce more devils like himself?!" I exclaimed frightfully.

"We don't really know *how* they got there but we do know that Oersted cares for them and calls them his daughters." I thought about this for a moment before Margret looked at Elizabeth and spoke.

"I say, they didn't look as threatening or devilish as Oersted to my eyes—are they girls like us, Elizabeth?"

"In some ways, yes, but in others, no. They don't do harm or enslave like Oersted does but they are made of the same demon flesh as he." We then looked back at the prison zone where Oersted was closing up the third box-hive that he had just extracted honey from. He then approached the Luna Hive with his tools, at which point we put aside the honey cells that we were sipping and focused our attention on him nervously.

Oersted stopped in front of the Luna Hive, knife in hand, and removed the stone block and lid. The inside of the box-hive was completely empty where even the devil-made wooden frames were missing. Surprised and increasingly enraged, Oersted threw his tools to the ground and lifted his massive leg up in the air. With a thunderous kick, the empty Luna Hive fell to the ground. The boxes separated and scattered on the dirt as Oersted then paced loudly over to the Meridian Hive. Because of our recent actions, the apple sauce dish was empty—Oersted noticed this. He swatted the dish to the ground and it cracked, spilling the gooey artificial nectar all over the dirt. Following this, the empty Meridian Hive met the same fate as the Luna Hive, tumbling to the ground and falling apart.

We looked on as Oersted's daughters fled into his lair through the door they exited from and closed it behind them. Oersted, the destructive demon, left the prison zone with his tools being pulled beside him. He threw his devices into his shed and then stopped for a moment. Where are my prisoners going, he presumably wondered. Then he looked toward the Grand Oak. We all tensed in fear as he slowly panned his focus up the tree from the bottom and noticed the way bees were swarming and working all around the branches. Oersted's face turned numb with malice. Oh no, I thought, we've been discovered! Oersted then looked down at the base of the tree again where the empty wooden frames were thrown by our bees who dismantled and abandoned them. He then scrunched his devil face and marched back into the lair.

We have to inform the Council, we all thought. As soon as the door closed on the Oersted Lair we rushed down toward the nest where apparently a casual, non-chalant meeting was being held. A crowd had gathered in front of the nest where Queen Luna was standing in front of Councilbee Andrea. Andrea was speaking happily to Queen Luna and the public crowd as we rushed through and stopped to listen.

"Do you, noble bee, affirm and avow that you will preserve, protect, and defend the Grand Oak as long as you shall live?"

"I do," answered Queen Luna steadily.

"Then by the power invested in me as Moderator of the Council, we grant you the position of Councilbee, to represent the bees you will govern while serving the greater good of beekind. Welcome to the nest—Oak be praised!"

"Oak be praised!" Councilbee Luna responded joyously as the crowd of her loving former daughters exalted her as a member of this different government that they now came to know and love. Meanwhile, the girls and I were trying to shuffle our way through the roaring crowd to get to the nest and inform the Council of the incident that we had just observed. But somehow, from behind the nest came another group of bees who apparently saw exactly what we did and began to whisper into Councilbee Andrea's ear. As the whispering ensued, the smile on Andrea's face disappeared as she became aware of what had just occurred.

Councilbee Andrea patted the whispering bee on the shoulder quickly and stepped back to tell Meadowlark. In an instant Meadowlark understood and leaped into flight, flying in circles around the Grand Oak to gather the entire populous to the nest for an emergency meeting. The bees naturally gathered quickly to Meadowlark's command and lined up on the Long Branch, nearly bending the wood from their collective weight. Meadowlark landed back in the nest and the informer bee was motioned to speak to the crowd, giving everyone the news firsthand.

"Just a few moments ago, the Oersted devil has found the Luna Hive to be empty and he has most likely come to realize that all of *'his'* bees are rallying on the Grand Oak." The bee delivered the news just as well as any of us could have while being shaken with nervousness. A few gasps and side-conversations rose from the crowd. There was no telling how this would affect the revolution. Meadowlark hastily stepped forward, for he knew that we always looked to him for his strong leadership, and that this was a fragile time for our society.

"Sisters, we must not panic! Instead we must ready ourselves to meet the changing tides of this revolution. The present plans to free the next box-hive must be put aside until we can guarantee there is no threat to the Grand Oak. Do not stir my sisters! All we must do is commence our great plans to assault the Oersted Lair presumably at the break of dawn tomorrow. As I have noticed, the new-bees from both the Meridian and Luna hives have not been sufficiently briefed on our specific plans to infiltrate the lair and destroy Oersted—but with proper training and Company assignment, our efforts will be successful. Now, our time is limited. The sun is falling, emergency training must begin at once, and all able-bodied bees that can fight *must* report to the High Branch at sundown where we will go over our leaf plans of infiltration and assault on the Oersted Lair." Then Meadowlark turned to the Councilbees beside him, pointing his beak at each of them.

"All Company Commanders will be stationed in the barracks to train those new-bees to be ready for battle and instruct them on where they will be placed in the battalion." Then Meadowlark looked at the nervously still crowd. "Get busy, bees, I want to start the briefing *precisely* at sundown—move!"

Every bee spread out and rallied to fulfill Meadowlark's commands. Following the Company Commanders, most of the bees flew down to the barracks at the base of the tree. Curiously, Councilbee Luna did not follow the others to the barracks. Perhaps she had only earned the status of Member of the Council and not the status of Company Commander, I thought. But then I saw her walk down the Long Branch into the newly built hives. My companions picked themselves up and headed to the barracks, but Harriet caught my eye as she passed me, following Councilbee Luna along the branch.

"Harriet, where is Luna going?" She turned to me with a strange calm smile.

"Councilbee Luna is in the process of laying new larvae in the newly built hives—that means younglings that will be born in freedom!" Harriet was excited and apparently unshaken by the hysteria over Oersted. Then, following the flow of the moving crowd, Harriet vanished to presumably assist the former Queen.

I looked around to find myself once again habitually tardy to the location of my friend's affairs, which at this point was in the barracks below the tree. I noticed the sun falling quickly out of the sky as I flew downward with the massive traffic of bees.

The barracks, filled with the vast swarm of bees, teemed with activity and hot sweat as many hustled about. Crawling through the cramped, heated tunnels I thought back to Rae, the bee Harriet and I had patched up. I remembered that she had told us she was a flapper who once kept the hive cool. Struggling to breathe through the tight passageways I wished so vehemently that she would flap her wings and cool down the barracks. Though I had the craving for this service, I knew deep down that it was part of the *old way* of doing things. Breaking from old traditions was always difficult, but absolutely necessary in the Grand Oak.

Companies were quickly segregated in the barracks and the new-bees were being assigned rapidly. I was sure glad to be under Andrea's command during these military exercises. After every bee was accounted for, we got right to work on flexing our wings, running laps through the tunnels to build up stamina, practicing using our stingers—which turned out to be quite a dangerous situation with some of the new-bees who had never been in combat before. I saw one bee almost pull out her entire stinger accidentally, just by stabbing the wax dummies.

I must say, at first my lack of faith in the new-bees was precariously high, but by the end of the day I knew that our Company Commanders would not let any of us leave those barracks without feeling comfortable that we would survive in a combat situation.

Training for hours left us dazed with exhaustion. However, the fatigue I had experienced from the training was undoubtedly nowhere near the magnitude experienced by the new-bees. We were tired but our stingers were sharpened, our minds prepared, and most importantly, our morale was high. Before long, it was announced that the assembly on the High Branch would begin in a matter of moments as the sky finally turned magenta from the sun's departure. We formed up in lines behind our Company Commanders and marched up the Grand Oak to the High Branch. I observed that the collective stomp of our large numbers in formation created a sound comparative to the massive steps of the Oersted devil. At last we are a somewhat formidable threat to Oersted, I thought.

The High Branch filled quickly. Meadowlark was standing with an impatient eye, glaring at all of us as we arrived. The Commanders, calm and collect as always, stood at the front of our lines waiting for the last of our comrades to fill in the empty spaces and be seated. At the moment we were ready, Meadowlark began the briefing with the leaf maps posted behind him.

"The Grand Oak does not possess the luxury of wings as we do, my sisters. Our home cannot simply fly away to a safer realm. That is why *we* are the caretakers for the Grand Oak. We must defend its holiness at all costs no matter what adversity we face. Without the Grand Oak we are nothing!" Meadowlark began pacing steadily back and forth.

"Because we have grown to be a large and prosperous population, we now pose a serious threat to the Oersted devil who has finally discovered us here. Most of you bees have been oppressed by this demon who wants nothing more than to see you placed in boxes again. Do you wish to be put in boxes?!"

"NO!" cried the bees.

"Do you wish to work to support the well-being of other demons like himself?!"

"NO!"

"Let us make a noise so vociferous that it disturbs the beast's slumber!"

"RAAAHH!" The entire crowd shook with wings fluttering, feet stomping, stingers rattling, and bees yelling. Our battle cry, fueled by our high morale, surely must have reached Oersted's ears, I thought while screaming loudly with my comrades. Meadowlark smiled.

"Now, my sisters, the time that we have all been waiting for is finally here!" Meadowlark stepped back to the leaf map depicting the layout of the Oersted Lair. "Here you can see that the Council has mapped out exactly where the three viable entrances are to infiltrate the lair; the chimney, the window sill, and the crease below the backdoor. The three divisions assigned to each entrance will infiltrate the lair in silence and with great cautiousness until all the Companies are inside. Then, we will locate Oersted's location among the various rooms and will attack before he can retaliate." Instantly a hand shot up out of the crowd from one of the warrior bees.

"But Meadowlark sir, how can we ensure victory over this terrible monster if our stings can only agitate him?" Meadowlark spontaneously formulated an answer.

"One sting may prick his skin, five stings may anger him, twenty stings may hurt him, fifty stings may numb part of him, but a thousand stings—a thousand stings will *kill* him!" The warrior sat down, reassured somewhat that his question was answered. Meadowlark paused for a moment, then resumed.

"Let me clarify something…This final revenge against your oppressor is *your* battle, my friends. This is your land. Once Oersted is out of the picture, we can move forward with restoring freedom to the last three imprisoned hives and repossess the land that has been taken from us by this devil. And this revenge will come at a high cost…" There were soberly grim faces all around.

"Many of you will not return to the Grand Oak tomorrow with your lives…those of you who sacrifice yourselves for your comrades and your home will live forever in the minds of the creatures you will save…Let me also make clear that I do not plan on returning with my life after tomorrow's assault." The audience was shocked. "I too seek revenge on this demon, for he has killed my family when I was but a chick…" For many bees, this was the first time they were hearing this. "Tomorrow I will enter through the chimney with that assigned division and quench my thirst for the blood of the devil as you, my sisters, will drink it too, and drink it well. I will not leave the Oersted Lair until my belly is filled with the demon's blood, my claws blunt from constant slashing, and my beak open holding the severed eye of the beast."

"Hurrah!" cried the bees. Then there was a profound mutual silence and we all looked around at each other and then back at Meadowlark who looked up at our faces.

"...There is no turning back...sleep well tonight, my sisters, we form up at sunrise—Oak be praised!"

"Oak be praised!" and the meeting was closed. Instead of rapidly exiting the High Branch, most bees walked with a strange somberness down the trunk, many contemplating the aftermath of the gruesome battle that would ensue at sunrise. I know that I was scared but excited all at the same time. I found Elizabeth walking down and I grasped her for a moment. We looked upon each other with upward-tilted brows of uncertainty, while still maintaining the sparkle in our eyes that was rejoicing to the simple word: *finally*!

We walked down to the Long Branch where we would retire for the night in our hive. But before entering the hive where I would sleep with my friends, I looked to the hive that I knew Harriet was situated in and approached it. I peeked into the small hive to discover Harriet sitting next to a comb of newly laid larva cells with a baby larva cradled in her arms. She was passionately rocking the baby to sleep when she noticed me and motioned for me to enter quietly. I was sensitive to my steps and sat down next to Harriet, looking at the adorable transparent white newborn larva.

"She's beautiful isn't she?" Harriet whispered.

"She sure is," I said. Then Harriet slowly placed the baby back into her comb cell and resealed the wax cap. We both said goodnight to each other and the babies sleeping in the comb and I returned to my sleeping quarters where I lied down beside my faithful companions and faded to sleep.

THE MORNING BEGAN WITH THE INFALLIBLE TICK-TOCK ascent of the sun into the sky. I had not slept well through the night, for nervousness grew swollen inside me. Waking up early, I arose from my crib to realize that my friends were already patrolling the Long Branch outside where apparently many sleepless bees like myself had risen earlier than normal. I stepped outside into the dim morning light and looked down the branch.

All was quiet on the Long Branch. A few bees passed by here and there, some grabbing honey rations, others flexing their wings in preparation for the inevitable. Other bees sat in wait by the edge of the Long Branch and on side-branches, just watching the ground. But most of the bees in the Grand Oak were still asleep. I noticed my friends watching the land from the side-branch quite calmly and diligently.

I approached Elizabeth, about to speak, but then suddenly everyone turned back to the farm where the Oersted Lair opened its mouth to release the demon. Every conscious bee on the Long Branch looked down and heard the slam of the door closing behind Oersted. He marched swiftly over to his shed and pulled out a

156

long wooden pole and his smoke spray cylinder. He then came straight at the Grand Oak as all the alert bees stumbled to awaken those bees still sleeping. Cries to attention rang out all over the Grand Oak. Bees were banging on hives anxiously to wake up their comrades. Instantly bees sprung out of their hives and looked around confused while other bees flew to other branches frantically. My companions and I rushed to the various branches, calling our sister bees to arms.

But it was too late. We could not awaken every bee in time before Oersted had reached the Grand Oak. We all looked down in terror as the devil lifted his wooden pole up to the branches of the tree and swung at the hives, shaking them out of the branches. With every whack from Oersted's pole, the Grand Oak shook as tremors sent shockwaves to hive foundations that caused them to fall right out of the tree. I lost my balance on the branches and was forced to remain in flight, barely dodging the leaves that swept by.

Hives were dropping to the earth, cracking into pieces on impact. The bees that survived the fall emerged from the broken hives agitated, only to be sedated by the smoke spray that Oersted puffed onto them from above. The situation was hopeless. Oersted's surprise attack disoriented all of us. And just before I thought that all was lost, that beautiful yellow-bellied, spotted-white bird launched out of the Grand Oak with immense speed right into the face of the devil. Meadowlark swatted at his eyes as Oersted was forced to drop his smoke spray machine and lose his grip on the wooden pole. The devil fought with his hands to try and shoo Meadowlark off of his face but to no avail.

I looked back and saw my sister bees forming into a wild swarm. We noticed Meadowlark's brave counter-attack which encouraged us to rally our spirits and charge straight at the beast. We jolted like wild savages directly at Oersted's flesh, grabbed on and refused to let go. Bees from the broken hives realized that they were not being repressed by the smoke spray any long-er and sprang up to pierce the skin of Oersted's legs.

Our numbers began to overwhelm Oersted. Little by little, Oersted's body was thickly covered with free-bees. Every inch of exposed flesh was laced in bees that began to scratch, bite, and sting the beast. Oersted could not stand the strain. He quickly ran like a coward back to his lair, crying in agony, louder and louder with every step. I latched onto a piece of clothing near the devil's chest. I hung on, desperately trying to crawl my way through his garments to reach his bare flesh. I looked up and was proud to see quite literally every single bee from the Grand Oak swarming around Oer-sted in a black cloud of vengeance.

The door to the Oersted Lair barged open. Oersted ran inside trying to get the free-bees off of him as we kept the door wide open for our sisters to join us in this bloodbath. Bees were already jabbing and implant-ing their stingers into Oersted, dying in the process. I didn't have a clear shot. Excitement and fear ran through my body as the bees who had released their stingers fell to the floor from the pain—the quite *neces-*

sary pain to ensure our victory. I could not wait. I was anxious to make my glorious thrust into the demon.

Inside the Oersted Lair I heard a slam as a door shut in another room. I could hear screaming and sobbing. It was Oersted's daughters locking themselves in a chamber unreachable by our comrades. As the battle ensued, more bees entered the lair from the chimney. They poured in and replaced the bees that had fallen to the floor. Oersted fell weak to his knees—shrinking to be much less colossal than he once was. Bees were climbing into Oersted's clothes, looking for fresh skin to sink their stingers into. I crawled up to Oersted's face and ended up on his rough pale chin. I tried to stab but the flesh was boney and I could not plunge deep enough to do any real damage.

I looked up at Meadowlark who had now firmly secured himself to Oersted's cheeks with his gripping claws. The blood dripped down from his nails. Meadowlark pecked at Oersted's eyes that suddenly caused the beast to grab hold of Meadowlark, drop his jaw open wide, exposing the dark red tunnel that was his throat. Instantly, bees flew straight into Oersted's mouth, down through his body to tear up his insides. I jumped at the opportunity and sank deep into the beast with my brave sisters.

All was dark. We felt our way lower and lower down. All around inside I heard the slashing of sharp stingers, cutting at the devil's organs. Soon there was a pool of red down below that echoed the gushing of blood, the squashing of organs, and the splashes of fallen bees who gave their lives for the glorious cause of freedom.

I threw myself against Oersted's slippery throat and sheared the surface with my stinger, sliding down, cutting the tube into two curtains of bloody demon flesh. I glided down with my stinger and reached a thunderously loud beating bulge. It was Oersted's heart! I could not slow myself down; the momentum from my descent was too great. I hit the beating heart and became stuck. My stinger became lodged and embedded in Oersted's main pump that propelled blood throughout his wicked system.

I heaved and heaved. I could not escape. My stinger was too deep in the beast. In fear of suffering the same fate as the bees who had fallen below into the pool of blood, I pulled hard one last time. With a crackle my stinger was discharged, completely disconnecting from my abdomen. My mouth opened wide as silent cries of pain tried to escape from within me. The pain was unbearably agonizing. My sharp stinger detached with a trail of my own blood streaming off where the umbilical cord was broken. My wings became weak; I was losing my grip and cried out for help. My hands slipped and I began to fall.

Then from above came a fluttering bee who jolted to the rescue and absorbed the shock of my falling body before it could reach the pool of blood at the bottom. It was too dark for me to see her, I could only feel her arms and hear her wings. She lifted me up and flew us both out of the Oersted devil.

Upon our exit, the bee flew me toward the open door where we had entered as I looked back at Meadowlark. Beholding the severed eyeball of Oersted, Meadowlark crunched it down with his beak until blood and ooze gushed out of the still moving eye. Meadowlark then persisted in devouring Oersted's bloody skull as he ducked his head through the bare eye socket and ripped out pieces of his brain. But with every peck, Oersted's hands gripped Meadowlark tighter and tighter, ripping feathers and crushing his bones. Oersted was about to collapse flat on the floor just as bees began to exit his body through his mouth, nose, eyes, and ears. The horrific sight disappeared from my vision as the bee carried me out the door of the lair and flew me toward the Grand Oak.

I glanced up at the bee who was carrying me and noticed that her body was cut in multiple places, her blood dripping slowly, her wings cut and punctured. I looked to her face and was stunned.

"Emily!" I cried. Her face was dripping with exhaustion. She not only was dealing with the pain of her own wounds but she was flying with me in her arms. We made it back to the Grand Oak but her wings finally exhausted the last of their strength and we fell to the ground below the tree where broken hives lay all around. Emily put my back up against one of the Grand Oak's massive roots and collapsed next to me.

We were both moaning from the pain we took on from our wounds. My body throbbed from my abdomen with blood pouring out profusely while Emily laid there panting as her body dripped blood all around. I looked around at the shattered hives. There were dead bees all around. Honey was spilt on the grass and dirt. Many bees wandered around, wounded and disoriented by the fallen smoke spray cylinder that still puffed bits of smoke at them as they walked. It was a brutal nightmare. Without much energy to speak, I turned to Emily who was sitting beside me, bleeding out as I was.

"W-what about th-the other girls?" I managed to say. Emily rolled her head over to me, her eyes soaked with tears.

"Ughh," She struggled to breathe, "Margret, Lynette, A-Anne...E-Elizabeth...all...dead!" She began to cry miserably as those same tears gushed out of my eyes.

"No!" I did not believe it. I *could not* believe it! I wheezed and retracted in another breath to speak. "...Harriet?" Emily shook her head loosely back and forth as the tears poured faster down my face. "N-No...I-I....*I*—" I was losing the ability to speak. My face was numbing from the loss of blood. Emily lost her speech too. The only conversation that carried on after that was spoken with rolling droplets of tears.

I threw my back up against the thick roots that supported my stiff body as I squirmed. Thoughts, memories, and worries all ran through my mind in every which way. *How* did they die? How *could* they die?! Were all of my companions lost in the fight? Did Oersted *really* die? How could we be sure? What will happen to the other three box-hives? Did we *fight* and *die* for nothing?!

These thoughts shook my mind. I could feel that I was about to die, slowly approaching death with each weak breath. I looked out to the expanse behind the Oersted Lair. Then out of the structure came Oersted's two beautiful daughters who ran out into the distance with joined hands, screaming. They ran and ran and ran some more. No bee went after them as they made their escape. The free-bees must have been too focused on devouring Oersted that they didn't even notice. The daughters dashed through the meadows without look-ing back—then they were gone.

My neck could no longer support my head. I in-voluntarily tilted my head back onto the root making my eyes look up to the Grand Oak where only a few hives were still intact from what I could see. I thought of the children, the baby larvae that were just brought into this world. Would they grow up and live in free-dom? Will they never know the suffering and oppres-sion of a box-hive? …Did they survive the attack?

I began to pray for them. Oh Grand Oak, I pray that their lives have been protected—secured by the newly built hives and combs. Please let me die knowing that we have saved a future generation of bees from slavery and death. Please, Oh Grand Oak, *Please*! Hear my plea!

The painful numbness began to consume my body. Oh Meadowlark—Meadowlark where are you?! I knew that he took a beating from Oersted during the battle—did his wounds only propel him to reap revenge on Oersted and then die with him? Could he even have survived? *Where are you, Meadowlark?!*

163

My eyelids began to weaken, bouncing open and shut by the weight of the last tears I managed to squeeze out. This was the end and I knew it. Why me, my bleeding body asked my mind. Because you chose this path, Shayla, my conscience answered.

My breaths became uneven. My heart was out of pace. My time was running out. With every slow blink of my bouncing eyelids the world around me began to melt. Reality was slipping. The blinks became slower and slower until finally there was no more strength to lift my eyes open and I was covered in endless darkness.

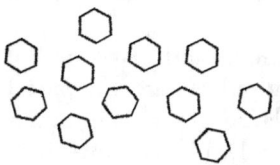

AWFUL SILENCE. COMPLETE DARKNESS. NO EARTHLY SENsations. All was still. But somehow my eyes started to open.

My eyes began to focus on what appeared to be a strange yellow mass in front of me. The blurry image began to sharpen. I was stunned! It was Meadowlark's yellow feather breast. He was standing right in front of me—unharmed, unscathed, untouched. Looking up at him; I saw that all his feathers were in place where they ought to be. Then he wrapped his magnificent white wings around me and picked me up gently. His feathers blanketed my skin. I could feel again!

He elevated me up and over his head where he placed me on his back right below the posterior of his neck. I compassionately held onto his soft feather body and sat. His wings sprung outward, showing the true length of his wingspan. With a whooshing sound, he leaped into the air above the roots of the tree and began to fly around the Grand Oak in circles.

The wind massaged my ears. Everything was peaceful. The ground was clean with the greenest grass I had ever seen. I had never flown like this before; I did not have to worry about supporting my weight or flying the right path—I was at liberty to simply view the world.

We circled the Grand Oak one last time and then Meadowlark flew out toward the pine forest. Crossing the meadow, I placed my arms around Meadowlark and hugged him sincerely. I loved him. He loved me.

Meadowlark flew above the great pine trees where the trunks came to dark green points at their tips. The canopy was a sea of green that waved to us as we passed by. Instead of stopping, Meadowlark flew slightly faster and faster, higher and higher! I looked down and saw the true scale of the pine forest which surrounded me. Meadowlark flew so high that I could even see mountains in the distance, white-water streams, and lush environments that I never knew existed. I realized that Meadowlark was taking me on a dream-flight at last. We kept flying as I began to feel the euphoric sensation of true freedom. And so we flew forever and ever into the great beyond...

THE END